THE LIVES LEFT BEHIND
TOVA AVIRAM-ZYLBERG

Producer & International Distributor
eBookPro Publishing
www.ebook-pro.com

THE LIVES LEFT BEHIND
Tova Aviram-Zylberg

Copyright © 2023 Tova Aviram-Zylberg

All rights reserved; No parts of this book may be reproduced or transmitted in any form or by any means, electronic or mechanical, including photocopying, recording, taping, or by any information retrieval system, without the permission, in writing, of the author.

Translation: Seree Zohar
Contact: aviramtova@gmail.com

ISBN 9798858670223

The LIVES LEFT BEHIND

*Historical Novel
Based on a True Story*

Tova Aviram-Zylberg

*This book is dedicated to my Father,
the Boy from Lublin,
who never ceased to love his city*

PROLOGUE

"Did I tell you the story about Yosseleh?" Herman, Talya's Abba, asked. "He was my sister Hava's oldest son, and I suggested they call him Yossef because I loved the Torah story about Yossef, and his multicolored robe, and the way he solved Pharaoh's dreams. My sister laughed and said that she actually loves the name too, and she just hopes that Yossef, or Yosseleh as he'd surely be nicknamed, won't have such big dreams!"

"Yosseleh was a highly gifted boy. Perhaps even a genius," he continued, stroking Talya's cheek. "He was the Polish chess champion for youth up to the age of thirteen. It's in our genes. We're the descendants of Rabbi Simha Bunim, from Przysucha. He was a very great Rabbi, but was also known as a brilliant chess player. Did you know that chess was also called 'Ishkuki' back in the eighteenth century? Maybe one day I'll teach you how to play."

Pulling the blanket up to cover Talya, Herman added that every time Hava would put Yosseleh to bed, she'd sing him a Yiddish lullaby about Yankeleh, whose eyes are black, and teeth so white. "*A yingeleh vass hat shoin alle tseyndalakh.*" A little boy who already has all his teeth.

Talya could see her Abba smiling at her through his tears.

YOSSELEH ZILBERMAN-KARLINSKI

Aged 5. One week after the Jewish festival of Simhat Torah, which ends the week of Sukkot. Corresponding to October 1930.

Today Stefania dressed me in an undershirt, a shirt, a sweater, and on that a white vest. Every time she dresses me in it, she reminds me that Mama knitted it specially for me because my eyes are black as coal. On top of all that she adds my coat.

"Mrs. Hava is nuts. She wants me to let you go into the zero degrees outside without enough clothes. She's got this psychosis about breathing fresh air all the time (I need to ask Mama what 'psychosis' means), not like the other zhid children in their closed-up homes that smell bad."

I already know that we're zhids. That's Polish for "Jews." But when Stefania says "zhid" or zhidowka" it sounds like she's patting my head. It's not at all like the way Igor says it. When he says, "Here's Yosseleh, the little zhid," he spits the words out, copying the way Vladek, who brings the wood, does. One time, a drop of spittle even landed on my cheek. I wiped it away quickly before Stefania could see and chase him with the stick she uses to push wood into the fireplace.

Igor's eyes are as blue as the sky sometimes can be. But not today. The sky today is not blue and I've already learned we can expect snow. I want tons of snow to fall. Then Mama, Tateh, and Braha will go into the yard and we'll build a great big snowman. "Run to Zalman the tailor," my Tateh will say to me in his deep voice, "and ask him for two buttons, black or blue or brown, or even green, for the eyes." (Why do the grownups always talk about the color of eyes?) "Zalman lives where the brown door is opposite our blue door. And ask him for a bit of red felt for the mouth. I'll get some carrot for the nose. We'll have the grandest snowman in all Lublin. In all of Poland! General Pilsudski will be very pleased. He'll say, "There's a good reason I love the Jews and granted them rights. It's because they build the best snowmen in the world."

Because it wasn't so cold yesterday, Igor came over to our yard and when Stefania wasn't looking he asked me to drop my pants. I wouldn't. He pulled out a small cake that his father had brought him. He told me it was the cake that the Madonna Maria Miriam gave Jesus to help him grow and become king of the Jews and savior of the world, but the Jews are so stupid that they don't understand how important this cake is because it gives boys really big dicks and it's important for a guy to have a big dick. So I let my pants down and he said that it's as he thought, that Jews have little dicks, and that his mother explained that the Jews cut off some of it, and she thinks some of them eat the bit they cut off.

Then he pulled his own pants down and showed me his, which had an extra piece that mine didn't. I told him that maybe his is big but Jesus, who they love so much and eat his cakes, had one like mine, and that cutting ours probably makes us really smart because everyone in Lublin, and where we live in Lubartowska Street in particular, says that the Jews are the smartest people even if they do have small dicks.

We could hear Stefania coming so we quickly pulled our pants up. Igor started running so she didn't manage to thwack him with the stick she uses to poke the wood into the stove, where it gets black from the fire. Sometimes when Mama kisses me she says to me in Yiddish *"Meineh schwartzeh oigelekh, di vist Yosseleh, di vist meineh neshumeh."* My little black-eyed Yosseleh, you are my soul.

I don't want to play with Igor and decided to wait for Christina. She arrived in her red coat and red hat. I ran to greet her.

"Look what I brought," she said.

She sat on the crate next to our snowman and opened a small tin box. Inside were buttons. Two medium sized blue ones.

"These are like your eyes. Maybe we can change the snowman's eyes to these," I suggested, smiling.

"Here," she said, "look, I've got a lot of brown buttons like your eyes and your mother's and your father's. We can give Tomasz different colored eyes whenever we want."

"Huh? Who's Tomasz?"

"It's your snowman. Let's pretend he's our child and we need to give him a name, like they gave my new brother in church. The priest recited the blessings from Jesus Christos and Madonna Mary, and then signed a cross on his face, and then said the baby would be called Lech, which is the name of an important man who invented our country, Poland."

"So is your baby brother's name Lech Pyotrowski? That's a funny name!"

"But Yosseleh Zilberman is funnier," Christina laughed.

Christina and I played at changing our snow-child's eyes until I heard Stefania calling. "Yosseleh, Yosseleh, come on home now."

Christina hugged me tight. "We'll get married," she whispered before I dashed indoors.

My grandfather lifted me up. His cheek was warm, and his beard tickled my face. "Playing with the shikseh again?" he laughed, using the Yiddish word for a non-Jewish girl.

I love my Zeideh, which is Yiddish for grandfather. My Zeideh Moisheh. He tickles me if I doze off while we're reading. Today we're reading the first story in the Torah because last week it was Simhat Torah, the festival we celebrate each year when we read the last part of the entire Five Books of Torah and on the same day, start again, reading the entire Torah again in sections during the coming year. To celebrate the ending and restarting, we sing and dance with the Torah scrolls in the synagogue Zeideh leads. It's the most beautiful synagogue in all Lublin, with massive golden chandeliers. Today we'll read the first section of Genesis.

Before going to synagogue on Simhat Torah, Zeideh gave me advance warning. "You know, Yosseleh, tonight all the synagogues in Lublin will be packed to full capacity, not just our synagogue in Gesia Street, because we'll not only be celebrating Simhat Torah but your birthday too!" Zeideh was laughing, teasing me.

"There are two times in the year when all the Jews, even those who read the 'Lubliner Shtimeh,'" Zeideh said, referring to the newspaper printed by Poland's completely secular Jewish population, "and those who studied in the non-Jewish universities in Polish and think they'll understand who created the world and why from books about the world or gravity or electricity, even they come to synagogue on Yom Kippur, when we fast all day and make a reckoning of our behavior with each other, and on Simhat Torah. They love coming to synagogue to dance with the Torah scrolls. The concept of starting again appeals to them."

My Zeideh Karlinski is the Rabbi of the Gesia Street shule, as we call the synagogue in Yiddish. "Until Yosseleh is six years old," he told Mama, "I'll come every day to teach him how to read Torah. He's a great treasure, that child, he'll become a luminary even before he's in kheider."

I already knew that kheider is the school where we study only Jewish texts. Mama always said Zeideh is a different kind of Rabbi, like our great-grandfather Rabbi Simha Bunim of Przysucha, who was a very great leader with hundreds of adherents. Sometimes he dressed like the Poles and set off for the markets in Lublin. He also played chess at some of the inns, and helped people who needed medicines because he was a pharmacist. If he found out about a Jewish girl doing things not appropriate to a Jewish life, he would invite her to his home where his wife would give her a warm meal, and water to wash herself in, and a bed with crisp clean sheets and a feather pillow, and let her sleep well. Then the young woman could decide if she wanted to go back to using the city baths, or let the Rebbetzin, as the Rabbi's wife is called, find her a nice Jewish family who needs someone to help them in the house or look after the children.

My Zeideh's face lit up like the angels in Christina's picture book when he smiled. But I know I shouldn't say that.

"Let's get started, Yosseleh," Zeideh said, settling me next to the brown table covered in a large slab of glass. He gently placed a Torah scroll down on the tabletop. The scroll smelled of the fragrant spices we used for Havdalah, the blessing we say when Shabbat comes to an end on Saturday night. The scroll was encased in a golden cover. Then he picked up the silver pointer, because we never touch the scroll with our bare hands. Doing that can damage the parchment. He pointed to the first word.

"Well, Yosseleh, my little luminary who knows how to read so nicely..."

And I began to read. "In the beginning, God created the heavens and the earth. And the earth was wondrously formless..." I stopped and gazed up at Zeideh. "What does wondrously formless mean, Zeideh?"

6 August 1936

Today I'm going to the chess tournament in Warsaw. I'd already traveled beyond Lublin with my grandparents to their holiday home in Zakopane. Every summer we took the train to Krakow, where Yanek Kojinski waited for us at the station with a large carriage, ready to bring us to the house. My sister Braha, who at home we all called Brahaleh, and all our cousins went there for the fresh air in the Carpathian Mountains. Bobbeh, which is grandmother in Yiddish, always said that it helps prevent coughs in the winter. But I also went in the winter vacation.

Yanek was also a ski guide. His father and my Zeideh would play together as children, and once even got caught in a snowstorm and spent the night at Yanek's grandmother Maria's house. The next morning Zeideh's parents came with the police looking for him. Yanek's mother said that she never slept that whole night. She wondered if his parents would still let him come skiing, because it was a sport that the non-Jews enjoyed. But my Zeideh's father just said that in the end it would all blow over.

"She'll calm down," he said quietly of his wife, "because even in the book that Rabbi Simha Bunim wrote, it says very clearly that a healthy body is the precondition for a healthy soul and mind, which are vital for in-depth study of Torah, because God would not have created mountains for their beauty alone. He created them to bring goodness to mankind."

Braha and the cousins loved going there in summer, but I loved the winter more because of the skiing and also because, before they all showed up, I had time alone to travel with Zeideh to Krakow, where he'd buy "products," which is how Zeideh called all the food we'd need for the vacation home.

Down in the basement were hooks hung with cleaned intestines. Yadwiga, the housekeeper, would make stuffed kishkeh by filling them with a mixture of fat and bread crumbs. This was added to the stew, called cholent, cooked in a massive pot and served only on Shabbat.

I'd never joined a competition where children from all over Poland were participating. "I'll take him to the tailor to order a new suit specially for the competition," my Tateh said. But Mama told my father that it wasn't necessary, that it was customary for a nice Jewish boy to get his first suit for his bar mitzvah, his coming of age ceremony at thirteen years old, and a nice white shirt and long navy pants would be sufficient, especially since they could be worn when other Jewish festivals were being celebrated.

I could hear Braha's quick steps approaching. She flew into the room and began screeching at our father. "I hate you and your little genius and the way you constantly dance around him just because he's going to a chess tournament! And can read from the age of three, and can add up fast in his head, and wants to be a brain research doctor. And I want what you promised me! A new dress for Rosh Hashanah!"

Rosh Hashanah, the Jewish New Year, was still a long time away, but I heard Tateh answer her calmly. "You'll get your cousin's dress."

"And it's practically new," Mama added.

Braha drew close and hissed at me that I'm just like Joseph of the dreams, that in the end everyone will hate me, and I won't have a good life if I keep on thinking I deserve to be given everything. I went downstairs to the garden. Christina wasn't there anymore.

Even though Mama told me that Braha is at an age when girls get really annoyed very easily and I should leave her alone, there was a lump in my throat. I noticed that Mama called her "Braha" instead of the diminutive "Brahaleh," a sure sign that Mama was angry too. But Mama hugged me, stepped back, took one look at me and immediately hooked me up to the inhaler to help me breathe.

The next morning, before our trip to Warsaw for the competition, I walked with Tateh for morning services at Zeideh's Gesia Street shule. Everyone there wished me success. After prayers were over, I said a private prayer to God: that my family all be well, and all Lublin's Jews too, because lately there'd been several anti-Semitic incidents from Polish people attacking our community, and even murdering three Jewish shopkeepers from Lipowa Street, but I wasn't concentrating well because my mind was busy thinking about Christina.

When Tateh gets angry about that I hear him saying "Yosseleh is with that shikseh again," but Mama reassures him. "Avrom," she says, "they were born at the same time, and her parents are our neighbors. She and Yosseleh are like brother and sister. What are you so afraid of? That he'll marry her? He'll be off to Yeshiva soon and won't even have time to see her anymore," she reminds him, talking about the school and seminary where Jewish students immerse only in Bible studies.

Tateh gazed at the medal all the way home from Warsaw. It was gold, and embossed with a chess knight. "First Place in the Chess Competition for Children under 13" was also engraved on it. That Friday night at the Shabbat meal, Zeideh spoke about modesty, the most important trait clever people must cultivate especially when they are awarded prizes. "Do not become haughty, Yosseleh," he smiled at me. But I just wanted to know if Christina had already heard of my win.

On Shabbat morning I looked out the window and saw Christina sitting on the bench we called ours, so I went down into the yard and slipped my hand into hers.

"Champion of Poland, smartest in the world," she said, "I understand that perhaps we'll never talk again."

My heart raced so hard that I could almost feel the lump in my throat choking my air. She said she'd heard my father saying that I'm too old to keep playing with her, that she knows I'll be sent far away to study, and that for sure we won't be able to talk. I said that we're friends for life and no one has any idea what could happen three years from now: there could be an earthquake or the Vistula River might flood Poland and there could even be a war and I'd die.

"Jesus-Maria, why do you talk like that, Yosseleh? Sometimes I think my father's right when he says you might look like a little boy but inside you're really an old man."

I laughed. My whole body shook from laughing. Christina laughed so hard that tears sparkled in her blue eyes. It couldn't be true, I felt sure, that anyone would try to separate Jews from non-Jews. I also knew that I loved Christina more than anything in the world and one day I'd tell Mama that, even though Tateh once said I should never make Mama angry because she almost died while giving birth to me. Every time Tateh told me that, I'd ask him to tell me the story. He'd lift me onto his shoulders but say nothing.

On the day we traveled to the tournament, he said it was very strange but to this day he can smell the stew of chicken necks with hints of cinnamon. It had been on the stove when Stefania's sister had come running to bring him home from shule. "Hurry, quickly," she said. He remembered making it home within five minutes and hearing Stefania say that everything was alright at first, that Mrs. Hava had even sat on the brown chair with a feather pillow ready to help ease her backache, and that Stefania shouldn't get upset or call Tateh home because things would be just fine.

Gazing through the train's window, Tateh stroked my head. "You came out with a head full of black hair like spikes and a beautiful, clean face. Stefania's sister bathed you and wanted to have me called home so that I'd know you were born. But a lot of blood kept gushing from Mama. Something inside had gone wrong.

Christina's parents heard her screams and quickly came over, wrapped her in several blankets, carried her downstairs to the wagon and took her to the Jewish hospital not far from us. Mama was already so pale that everyone was sure she wouldn't come through it. 'Our little orphan,' Stefania kept calling you."

In the hospital, which Tateh always mentioned was the most sophisticated in all Poland, having been built in 1886 by the wealthy Jews formerly of Lublin but now living in America, although they never forgot their city of birth, Mama was checked by the new x-ray department and settled in one of the special beds for women with post-natal complications. They cleaned her well and gave her a blood infusion. Two weeks later she was back home.

Stefania's sister had also just given birth so she breastfed me too. Mama couldn't, even after she was back home. Stefania said Mama was saved not only by virtue of Stefania's prayers to Jesus and Maria but also the candles she lit for the saints. And after that came the winter which was so cold that even the old time Lubliners could never recall such a thing.

"We kept the stove running the whole time," Tateh recalls. "It kept our room warm because your crib was there and we were so afraid you'd freeze to death the way Zalman the tailor's son did in the harsh winter of 1929. They found him the next morning, blue and purple, not breathing, and unable to be resuscitated."

Tateh looked out through the window at how quickly everything seemed to pass by. We'd just gone through the Kazimierz Dolny train station, and I knew that any moment now Tateh would tell me again about the great king of Kazimierz who loved the Jews so much that he drew up a bill of rights in 1364. Tateh would recite those rights because he knew them rote.

"The king accepted the request of Jews settled in cities throughout the kingdom of Poland, since he was keen to increase his treasures. He therefore granted them the right to dwell and move about freely in the kingdom, to trade, and to import and export merchandise, as well as the right to grant loans for interest in the form of pledges and mortgages."

Tateh also told me that Kazimierz loved Esterkeh, a Jewess, who saved the Jews when the Poles wanted to kill them by asking Kazimierz to build the Jews a specially dedicated area in Krakow, the capital city, which the king did.

I kept thinking that if Kazimierz loved a Jewish woman so much, then I could love Christina. I know that several years from now I'll tell my parents that I love my neighbor and friend, and I don't care whether she's a shikseh or not. If Tateh talks about Mama's difficult time when I was born, then clearly the people who saved Mama were Christina's non-Jewish parents. Oh, and the person who fed me and kept me alive was none other than non-Jewish Stefania's sister.

YOSSELEH
June 1938

As I traveled with Tateh to Warsaw for the tournament, I realized that I'd never forego my friendship with Christina. Yes, I'd continue preparing for my Bar Mitzvah: I wouldn't want to disappoint Zeideh Karlinski and the whole family. But even before I reached thirteen I attended an activity by the Socialister Kinder-Farbend, the Children's Socialist Association, known by its initials, SKIF.

Preparing for my bar mitzvah meant learning the weekly Torah section from Genesis, and the reading from the Prophet Isaiah. They brought dormant questions to the surface: why do we put our faith in God when there are starving people in the world, when there's so much loathing and violence towards Jews even though Jesus was Jewish, and so on. I had plenty of questions, which made me think that people need, and must take, actions to improve their own destiny in this world, and not just rely on prayer.

Stefania's son Igor, older than I, told me about a Jewish youth movement which belonged to the "Bund." The Bund was the Jewish Labor Party. Igor's father, who my own Mama called "Mr. Pozner," was active in the

Polish Socialist Party, also called PPS. It looked after the poor, and worked in conjunction with the Bund organization to improve the lives of laborers. Igor told me very excitedly how his father organized the leather industry laborers' strike.

"Preparing the hides for sewing coats and shoes is really hard work," Igor said.

"And stinky," I added, thinking of the tanning process.

"Yes! They work and work and some still don't have enough to eat. The strike was together with the Jewish laborers, who were organized by the Bund. You won't believe it, Yosseleh, but they actually gained improved work conditions and even a raise in salary."

When Igor gazed hard at me, his eyes shone. "You're always telling me about poor people you meet when you walk with your Zeideh Karlinsky to shule. So obviously just praying doesn't help."

He gave me a printed page that announced a gathering for children aged eleven to thirteen, scheduled for the coming Tuesday. Everyone would play games together and take part in SKIF youth activities run by the Bund. I decided to go.

Entering the Culture League building and going to the room where the SKIF children would meet, I could feel how different this place was from everything I knew. It was like an island of freedom. Children were talking, expressing their views, laughing.

"Welcome, Yossi," Zelig the youth counselor said, using a more modern Hebrew form of my name. "We're talking, and primarily learning, about how to listen to each other."

Zelig lived not far from my street and knew I was Rabbi Karlinski's grandson but he presented me very simply by my first name. "Yossi wants to be our friend," he told the group.

After that I was on tenterhooks every week waiting for Tuesday to come around. I told Zeideh that I couldn't come on Tuesdays to study for my bar mitzvah.

"Why not?" He glanced up from the book he was reading.

"I'm staying back after school because the teacher asked me to arrange a chess group for younger children," I said, poker-faced.

Zeideh hugged me. "I'm not worried, Yosseleh. You already know the material perfectly. Giving of your time to train children in chess is no less important than learning the section from the Prophets."

I felt terrible about the white lie to Zeideh but it wasn't too far from the truth, because Zelig knew I was a chess player, that I'd won the youth tournament, and had indeed asked me to teach the game's basics to any interested group members.

Tuesdays. I love them. I love listening to the ballad that Zelig reads at the start of almost every group meeting. It's about Hirsch Lekert, a Jewish socialist activist. The ballad describes the First of May demonstrations of 1902 when Poles, together with Jews from the Bund, joined forces. The protest was suppressed by sword-wielding Cossacks under the command of Victor von Wahl, Governor of Vilna. Countless demonstrators were punished by public whipping. Hirsh Lekert, a simple shoemaker and member of the Vilna Bund, volunteered to kill von

Wahl. But after seriously injuring the commander, Hirsh was caught and hung in Vilna.

"This Jewish hero rose up to avenge the laborers' humiliation," Zelig said, and I knew I'd found my true friends, others like me who wanted a more just world and would work for it rather than merely wait for salvation. Zelig suggested I join the Morgenstern Sports Association, one of the largest in Poland. "Chess is a fantastic game, Yossi, and of course you're a brilliant player but you also have to build up your physical strength." I remembered the ski incident and Zeideh Karlinsky's approach. A healthy mind needs a healthy body.

"Maybe I can join the football team," I said.

"Training takes place in the big field a few minutes from here," Zelig smiled.

Igor told Christina that I was secretly joining Bund activities. When I went down to the yard I found her sitting on the stone in the corner where we always sat and chatted.

"All these things you're doing… And what if you get caught?" she said. "I don't want your grandfather Karlinski and Hava and Brahaleh and your father to hate me and my parents and think that what you're doing is because of me, because of any of us."

I gently stroked her hand where it lay on the stone.

"I love you, Yosseleh," she said, her sapphire eyes sparkling, "but my soul will never rest or calm itself if I make your family ostracize you, because I know how much they love you. Everyone, even Braha who's sometimes jealous, says things like "Yosseleh's such a great chess player," and "Yosseleh's the best student at school as well as in his Jewish studies" and "He has a heart of gold, he has deep wise eyes, he is…"

"Stop!" I said to Christina, squeezing her hand, perhaps a little too strongly judging by the way she flinched. "It has nothing to do with you, or perhaps it does, a little, because I know it's not fair for them to say that after my bar mitzvah I'll go to Yeshiva and forget you. I hear Mama saying it to Tateh, to calm him down. But mostly I've just stopped believing that there's a God who helps people. I stopped believing that God even exists in the form he's described. I love our songs, and the Torah, and stories, and even the discussions, the sharp minded arguments back and forth. But somewhere inside me I know that the Bund will save more of the miserable, poor people than God will."

He paused. "And in addition to that, do you have any idea what size library they have in the Culture League? Over three thousand books, and a reading room with newspapers from all over Poland and other countries abroad. And I'm going to start playing football."

I gazed into the bluest eyes in the world and suddenly burst into raucous laugher.

"Remember our Tomasz Snowman? And how we argued about what color buttons to give him as eyes?"

"The laugh of a hooligan and the hands of a pianist," Christina said, leaning her head on my shoulder.

I felt her hand relax inside mine and knew I'd managed to reassure her.

YOSSELEH'S BAR MITZVAH
October 1938

The watch tinkled. It was the same tone that came from the great Rabbi's pocket. That watch was passed down through the family. It used to belong to my great grandfather, Rabbi Simha Bunim.

"It's a very old watch which I kept specially for you, my dear grandson." Zeideh's eyes were moist as he handed the gold watch and chain over to me.

Usually I sleep later on days when there's no school. After the alarm rang, everything went silent again. I heard nothing, not even the birds chirping, until Zeideh's deep voice gently washed over me.

"My Yosseleh, my bar mitzvah boy, we learned about putting on the Tefillin." He was talking about the black phylacteries that Jewish males wear during morning services once they are thirteen.

"And we studied the section that you need to read from the prophets," he continued. "Today is 22 Tishrei 5699, your special day." That's my birthday according to the Jewish calendar.

So I got up and washed, the cold water sparking my body awake. Look what you're doing to Zeideh Karlinski, I berated myself. He so deeply anticipates that you'll do what's expected, always telling everyone how you'll be the one to take over from him.

The lump in my throat grew bigger. What if I choked while reading the Torah in front of everyone?

The suit stitched by Zalman the tailor hung on its special hanger near the bed. Next to it hung a crisp white shirt. On the shelf nearby was a large brown box holding my new black hat which Zeideh had ordered from the hatter in Warsaw. Tateh, Mama and Brahaleh stood at my door.

"Good morning, bar mitzvah boy!" they sang out in unison.

Mama came over and kissed my forehead.

Brahaleh laughed. "Get up already, little brother, prince of the Zilberman-Karlinski dynasty!"

My Zeideh is one of the visionaries behind the "Chochmei Lublin Yeshiva," a set of institutions which begins with preschool and goes all the way to special arrangements for married men. The Yeshiva teaches only Jewish studies, Torah, Gemarra and so on. In the famous photograph of its 1930 inauguration, Zeideh stands next to Rabbi Meir Shapira, head of the Yeshiva. During the past few weeks, as my bar mitzvah approached, Tateh said the same thing to me many times. "Yosseleh, you will study in this wonderful Yeshiva's sixth cycle of students which is restoring Lublin's status as the most important center of Jewish learning in all Poland. It only accepts the smartest students, and you'll be among them."

Of course no one in the family had an inkling about my plans, but I knew that this bar mitzvah would be my parting gesture. After that, I'd be crossing the bridge, so to speak, to the other side. I don't plan on attending the Chochmei Lublin Yeshiva. Instead, I'll join studies at the Shofar High School, because I want to be part of the Haskalah movement, the "enlightenment," in which Jews integrate into the big wide world. Jews like Albert Einstein, who I read about in the Culture League's library and who, as early as 1905, already published important articles on physics. I also read about Zigmund Freud, a famous doctor who worked at assisting people with emotional and psychological problems by talking with them at length and through hypnosis. I think I'd like to be a doctor.

But for now, I'm trying to push these thoughts aside as I walk with Zeideh and the family down Gesia Street to the shule. There used to be a very famous building next door to it, the "Four Countries Committee." It was the most important Jewish judicial institution but it was destroyed in the big fire of 1655.

I'm about to celebrate my bar mitzvah, to put on the Tefillin properly for the first time with the blessings, because until now I only practiced without the blessings, to become one of the Jewish men who read the eternal words of Torah. I must say that the portion of Genesis I get to read is very powerful. The one G-d, the Creator of the Universe, puts our world together over six days, and sets the first human in it. "And G-d created mankind, man and woman he created them," and imbues them with the ability to apply morals that differentiate them from every other living creature and allows them to discern between good and evil. The righteous will be rewarded, the evil will be punished, our Sages teach.

But where does that actually exist? Perhaps the Bund will help other simple, honest folk receive a little more, just as the tanners and leather workers did after their strike.

Entering the shule, I say the opening prayer and carefully put on my new Tefillin. My family and the congregation watch, their eyes sparkling with joy. Mama wipes her tears away with a pristine white kerchief. I chant the Torah portion loudly, clearly, and end with the section from Isaiah.

"May the heavens hear and the earth take note," Isaiah says, predicting destruction, which I know is coming because Germany has a new leader who screeches his political views in stadiums. Pretty much all he talks about is destroying the Jews.

I move the pages on which I wrote my speech a little further aside. I don't need them. I know the material well.

"A question was put to Rabbi Simha Bunim," I begin, about to explain a point of Jewish thinking. I hear the congregation sigh in approval. "Would you want to be in our forefather Abraham's place? Rabbi Simha answered no, he wouldn't want to be. What advantage would it be to G-d, of blessed name, if Abraham could be me or I could take over his role?"

And I continue to expound on how all people are different from each other in their natures, each of us must find our own way, and that is where the greatness of humanity lies.

"This is what Isaiah 1:15 says: 'When you spread your hands forth, I will hide My eyes from you; verily, when you make many prayers, I will not hear; your hands are full of blood.' We read how the Prophet rejects glorifying actions that are actually empty of real content as long as justice is not being done. He is deeply disturbed by the moral deterioration which continues to develop in Jerusalem."

I talk on, then close my discussion by thanking my family for teaching me to love my fellow man. I turn to Zeideh who is smiling broadly, his eyes showing joy and sorrow. "Thank you, Zeideh, for teaching me the interpretations of our great ancestor Rabbi Simha of Przysucha, of whom it is said that he was not only well versed in the Hassidic ways of life but also in the enlightened ways, as they're called. He read all kinds of books, played chess with all kinds of people, and even attended theater. They say it was one of his ways of bringing those who lost their way back to the paths of Jewish tradition. I know that you, and in your footsteps, I, too, highly appreciate his openness and the way he paid the same attention to the poor as to the wealthy, to the young as to the elderly, all receiving the same warmth and love."

I glance up, noticing a flash of sorrow in Zeideh's eyes. He understands.

"Our dear boy," Zeideh hugs me after I step down from the dais. "Our dearest Yosseleh, our genius, the heir to Rabbi Karlinski…" people variously say as they shake my hand and congratulate me.

Brahaleh comes down from the upstairs women's gallery, pushing her way through the men, and kisses my cheek. "What a man you are, equal to all others!' she whispers in my ear but what I catch is a whiff of scent, which is just like Christina's who, after washing her hair, sometimes comes outside to sit with me in the yard on our favorite block of stone.

"What's that perfume?" I ask my sister.

"I took some shampoo from Christina," she laughs, and I feel as though I'm growing wings, flying out and away from the congregation and their hugs and well-wishes right into the delicate sweetness of a faint sweat mixed with tobacco and goose fat and ancient pages of Torah books, I'm flying towards the sun hoping my wings won't melt as Icarus' did, which I know because Zelig, the Bund counselor, told us the story.

March 1941

I stayed with Mama in our home's basement, in the pit which Tateh and I dug behind the big cupboard more than two years earlier on the day after we heard planes flying in circles overhead, and missiles blasted into Lublin. We had enough time to set up a kind of bunker that we could not only sit in, but also lie down in. The exit was accessed by a ladder into the large cupboard, which Zeideh called "the products" cabinet. A pantry of sorts. Two weeks after the first bombs fell, we heard boots stamping and shouts.

"Achtung! Achtung!" Attention!

It was clear: Lublin had been conquered.

Tateh disappeared nine months ago when he went out to find water. Christina said that she checked the Judenrat offices, the organization representing Jewish affairs in Nazi occupied areas. She spoke to Mark Alten, who used to frequent Rabbi Karlinski's home. Mark said that Tateh had been taken to the forced labor camp in Lipowa 7, and that no one should worry because he's strong and can do physical work, and in any event this whole craziness would pass once England came to Poland's assistance, because there was a mutual protection agreement between the two countries.

I could see in the sky-blue of Christina's eyes that everything she was telling us was meant to reassure Mama but I knew that I no longer had a Tateh.

I managed to take the chess set down into our bunker and most of the time played against myself, thinking how fortunate it was that Zeideh, Bobbeh and Brahaleh had gone to Zakopane towards the end of August. Maybe they'd had enough time to escape. Maybe they even found a better hideout than we had.

Mama and I have already spent six months in the bunker. Christina brings us scraps from her family's meals. Mama tells Christina that she shouldn't, they barely have enough for themselves. Then Christina's eyes fill with tears and she says that we're now part of the Pyotrowski family.

She sits on the tin bucket that contains our bedpans, which she carts outside to empty and brings back towards evening.

"Governor Ernst Zörner has announced that a ghetto will be set up in Lublin, in the citadel sector near Growdska Street. Polish families have just been evacuated from their homes and the order is that by 24th March, in other words, two days, all the Jewish families still in Lublin must move to the ghetto."

Christina snorts in a way that's very familiar to me. When we used to play together, running around, and suddenly she was out of breath, she'd let out this snort and we'd both burst into laughter. She tries controlling her breathing.

"I think you should leave this hideout and move to the ghetto, because Polish families will move here instead, turn the place upside down looking for valuables, and find you here," she said.

"The pill you brought me from Chemist Podolski really helped calm me," Mama tells Christina. Mama smiles. "Of course he added a note saying that our lives are in the hands of Jesus and Maria, and that he is not permitted to give me the pill I requested, but I reminded him that Rabbi Karlinski's permits for a pharmacy greatly assisted in getting him accepted by the Jewish Health Organization in Poland, which the Rabbi helped establish in 1923. That must've helped him decide to take care of me, and now I'm fine. I do have one request though, Christina. I know it's close to impossible but I'm begging you: do everything to save our Yosseleh."

Christina cries as she hugs me. I kiss her face, and lick the tears. Mama doesn't care anymore that I feel the way I do about a shikseh. And it's clear G-d couldn't give a damn. I love my Christina more than ever.

"We'll go to the ghetto. It'll release you from all this danger," Mama says.

"I'll look after you in the ghetto," Christina nods. "I've already organized my entry permit through my job at the municipal sanitation department. Pretty much every day I'll be accompanying workers who need to fix the sewer in Gesia Street."

"An interesting job," I say and Christina smiles, but it's a smile steeped in sadness.

Christina gives me a bag with a crimson sweater that her mother knitted. "Lech grew so fat that even though he's younger than you, this sweater's small on him already. It'll help keep you warm," she says, wrinkling her little nose.

That's another gesture I know so well from as far back as when we built Tomasz the Snowman. I turn my face towards the wall so she won't see the tears in my eyes and be even more upset. But I know she sees them through my back, so to speak.

When we get to the ghetto, I'm thrilled I've got this warm sweater even though spring is fast approaching. It's still quite nippy outside.

YOSSI in the GHETTO and the FORTRESS
24 March 1941 – 11 April 1944

Christina comes into the ghetto three, sometimes four, times a week by virtue of her job, bringing me half a potato, a half or quarter loaf of bread, and sometimes a small piece of meat. She slips these things out from under her loose blouse. "Here, for you," she says. And I hear Zeideh's voice whispering in my mind that the Holy One, Blessed be He, doesn't mind that you're not eating kosher food right now; he cares only about being sure you have the strength to get through this ordeal of 'Binding of the Jewish People.' I whisper back, as though to Zeideh, or perhaps to G-d who I don't believe in, 'And where is the ram for a sacrifice?'

"Did you say something, Yossi?" Christina asks. She stays with me for five, occasionally seven, minutes. I want to kiss her sparkling blue eyes non-stop, her nose, her mouth, her earlobes. We're sitting on the floor. She holds my hand.

"What's with Ludwig?" she asks.

"I'm still his chess slave."

"Excellent!" She kisses my neck, stands, straightens

her green skirt, ties her scarf over her golden curls, and says she's got to leave.

Every day Ludwig Schmidt sends his secretary out to bring me into the Gestapo office. "What immense fortune it was that Dr. Mark Alten," he's referring to the Judenrat head, "told me about you, Yossi Zilberman."

That's how he prefaces every chess game against me. Then he goes on to say that he could never imagine such a thing as a Jewish boy being Poland's Youth Chess Champion.

"I wrote to Marta that I'd found a challenger to play against and she's a bit concerned about the influence which you, as a dangerous Jewish worm, might have on me." He laughs raucously and slashes the floor with the black whip always in his fist, even when we play.

"I don't belong in this place," he adds. "I was fine managing the Gestapo office in Heidelberg. I studied in the oldest university in Germany, the Ruprecht-Karl in Heidelberg, founded by Ruprecht the First in 1386. You get that, Yossi? You get that it's highly inappropriate for me to even smell the zhids, which pop up from every wormhole in Lublin?"

His whip slashes the floor again.

"But what can we do when you're called to the office of the Gestapo commander Miller, and he himself requests that you assist in handling the problem of the Jews in Lublin? Your own people, Yossi. Can one decently refuse Miller, who is himself still in an emotional tangle because his patron, Heidrich, was murdered by those Czech pigs? Can one, Yosseleh? Is it at all possible?" He screeches, punctuating his rhetoric by repeatedly slashing the whip. "No. I don't belong in this place. I'm just doing my work. But I'll do it the best I can."

"Can I show you an interesting strategy known as the Scholar's Mate?" I ask, trying to distract him from the repetitive remarks about his miserable life in his current position as deputy to Herman Werthof, Gestapo Commander of the Lublin Ghetto.

"You're lucky that you play chess, Yossi. Yosseleh, as the zhids call you. Otherwise you'd long since have ended up like so many other Jews around you and in the ghetto: ground meat." He laughs, bringing his face close to mine, tapping his cheek with his finger to signal that I should take a whiff. "A pleasant smell of soap. Yes?"

I nod.

"You've got to admit that they smell pretty bad. They stink, your mates. I don't understand it. It's the stench of their rotten skin and blood, or the garlic and onion they gobble up."

And I'm thinking that since my fellow Jews have just about no food at all, their skin has the smell of death.

"Do I amuse you? I saw a smile."

"No, Herr Schmidt. It's not funny at all. Would you like to practice this move in three stages? Here. The king's pawn moves two squares forward..."

"I heard they caught your grandfather in Zakopane. See, Yossi? I take a deep interest in you. He hid with your grandmother in Yanek Kushinski's shed. That Pole begged that no one hurt the Rabbi and his wife, and he even said that they'd already lost their daughter in the bombings at the start of the war, and he also said that he'd be willing to go with SS Officer Meier instead of the Rabbi. So Meier shot the stinking Pole."

Schmidt tut-tutted, shaking his head. "Your grandfather begged them not to touch his beard. Nor did he obey Meier's order. And what did Meier request? Nothing more than to show him how to light a cigarette on your Sabbath."

For a while now I can't feel my body.

I'm stone.

Maybe I'm dead.

I'm not dead.

I hear Ludwig. "Meier is an excellent officer. A relative of mine. He's not called Schmidt because he's from my maternal side. He's Meier, a name that sounds Jewish, true, but he's pure Aryan. He asked the Rabbi how this God who abandoned them looks."

I can't feel my body at all. I'm wondering if death has at last come to redeem me, but it seems I just fainted, because I woke on the floor in the room adjacent to Ludwig's office. And suddenly I think about the future, about how I'd like to study the human brain, how it can invent so much evil.

That's what I'm thinking about right now.

I'm thinking about the future, and life, and how death could save me. That's what I think about when I know how they tormented my Zeideh Karlinski who did only good in this world.

That's what I think about when I'm actually not even thinking about much.

And I think about Christina.

"When I no longer exist you'll remember our

breathing together, our embrace, our laughter, my little sanitation expert," I laugh when we're seated next to each other on the floor, holding hands.

"You'll live, Yossi," she whispers. "The Soviets are advancing, getting closer. You'll live and study medicine and research the brain and you'll be an important doctor and scientist. And a great chess player."

"A small one," I say and she laughs, her blue eyes sparkling and dropping tears.

I want to kiss her without ever stopping, stroke her face, her eyes, her nose, her earlobes.

The only time I can breathe is when you're with me.
Silently.
Without talking.
Disconnected from the world.

Screaming. Crazy Zusha's screaming, running around the ghetto in her torn dress, her breasts exposed, raising her arms upwards, laughing loudly. Standing around in a circle is a group of whistling, laughing soldiers. A shot rings out. Christina and I peek from the window. Ludwig, in his gleaming boots, gun in hand, stands over Zusha's body.

"The show is over!" he screeches and cracks the whip. "Schnell!" he yells. The soldiers leave.

"I've got to get you out of here at least for a few hours so you can breathe. Properly. Fill your lungs," Christina says.

"But I'm Ludwig's chess slave," I laugh, and for a moment we're both back in the yard building Tomasz, and Mama's coming out to bring us biscuits and explaining how healthy it is to play outside and breathe fresh air.

"What's with Mama?" I ask. Ludwig had told me he's taking care of her, that she's in hospital, and that she's showing signs of recovery from typhus, and the reason he's looking after he is because she's the mother of the zhid chess maestro.

"Rumor has it that the professionals and artists will be moved to the Lublin Fortress," Christina said, shivering. "Tomorrow I'll bring you another coat. This year the cold in November…"

"Is really cold."

She laughs, with sparkling tears.

"Every December when you build Tomasz before Christmas, you'll feel as though I'm stroking your cheek."

Once again she tells me that the Red Army is advancing and the Wehrmacht is on the retreat. She doesn't tell me that my mother was murdered in the Gestapo prison in the Fortress, in a comfortable room with an en-suite bathroom. And I was too afraid to ask. I knew but sort of didn't know.

"I couldn't save Mrs. Zilberman," Ludwig tells me. "Stockmeister, the Polish sadist, shot her on Erntefest even though I told him she's under my patronage. Werthoff forbade me from getting rid of Stockmeister, saying he's one of the most effective officers around."

Erntefest. It means Harvest Festival in German. Christina told me that it's what the Nazis called the massacre of Jews on November 3rd in Majdanek. She shared this before the professionals and artists, as we were being labeled, were transferred to Mala Prevnost, or The Small Fortress, requisitioned as a Nazi prison.

"You didn't tell me," I sobbed.
She whispers. "I couldn't."
I hug her tight.

Not only did Ludwig Schmidt tell me about Erntefest but also that he'd be traveling home to Heidelberg for Easter. He was feeling very excited at reuniting with his family, and his beloved brother Heinrich, having not seen him since September 1939. He also said that he'd truly miss playing chess with me.

"But he also said, 'Look after yourself,'" Christina sniffled and smiled.

"Stockmeister the Sadist will be in charge of the Fortress prisoners, me included," I told Christina.

Every time Stockmeister walked past the chess table in Werthof's Gestapo command center and saw Ludwig busy playing, he'd sidle up close to me to threaten me. "I'll eradicate you. I'm just waiting for the moment Schmidt isn't around." He'd stand there for a moment longer, then go on his way, his snigger ringing in my ears and the beam of light reflected from his front gold tooth glinting in my heart.

"The Soviets are even closer. We just need a bit more patience, Christina encouraged. "I brought you a holiday dinner." She received a special permit to supervise waste removal following the festive meals eaten by the reduced Fortress staff kept on location to guard the prisoners.

"G-d won't let someone who plays chess so well and wants to study the human brain die right when the war is coming to an end."

"The only time I can breathe is when I'm with you."

"Yossi," she whispers in my ear, "my love, I know things aren't simple but when you, my scientist, talking about living without breathing, it's really troubling. We talked about you studying medicine in Warsaw."

I smile and kiss her eyes which envelope me in blue softness. Without talking, disconnected from our warped theater of the absurd, Christina removes her dress and I cover every spot of her body with kisses. Silently we make love as though the two of us are on fire.

"I'll die young. I want you to know, love of my life," I say, "that everyone has a soul which wanders the world. I'll always be with you. When someone touches your shoulder, just know that it's me. When the breeze lifts the ends of your curls, you'll remember me. When you swim in the Vistula, you'll feel me above you. When you build Tomasz with your children, I'll be there. You'll mourn, you'll be sad, but don't live your life in sorrow. Laugh, feel, talk to me. I'll be listening."

Christina kisses my eyes.

I close mine tight.

I'm flying I'm flying I'm flying I'm flying I'm flying I'm flying I'm flying far above Lublin and my Zeideh's house and Igor's house, far above Mama's brown eyes, flying like Icarus. Perhaps I'll reach Australia and hid in a pouch and they'll think I'm a joey rather than a Jew.

"Yosseleh, my Yossi, wake up," Christina shakes me, whispering.

I lick her tears. I know that Stockmeister the Polish sadist will kill me once he wakes from his celebratory Easter vodka stupor.

EDDIE (EDWARD) PERKINS' MEMOIRS
11 April 1953

When I played the animals-in-the-garden game with Granny, she couldn't find the critter I meant in the row of watermelon.

"The ladybut's here," I said.

"It's called 'ladybug,' Eddie," Granny corrected me.

Grandma Dolly is a teacher so I know that when she corrects my words, she's right. But I told her that I'm a teacher of all the countries in the world and I know how to say 'ladybut' in Hebrew, too.

"Why Hebrew all of a sudden?" Granny laughed.

"Because Rosa the kindergarten teacher has a book about colors and in Hebrew it's 'khipushit,'" I tell her.

Viki, the friend I meet in summers when I visit my grandparents in Sydney, doesn't know Rosa and doesn't want to learn words in Hebrew. Viki asks why I have a small bald spot on the back of my head.

"A piece of plasticine jumped out of the box and my mother cut my hair where it got stuck. Stop laughing!" I tell Viki, "it really did happen!"

"Plasticine doesn't know how to jump," Viki says. That's exactly what my mother said. It really annoys me because I have to insist to them that my plasticine does jump.

Viki's grandfather comes from a different country, called Poland. She told me that's why her name is Viktoria with a 'k' and she's called Viki for short. He keeps saying Dziękuję. It sounds like 'djenkooyeh.'

"Is 'dziękuję' a ladybug in Polish?" I ask Viki.

"Huh? No, of course not. It means thank you. My grandfather says it all the time, for anything. He doesn't have much food in 'Bidgosht.'"

"How come you invent such funny words?" I say, and hop around on one foot saying "bidgosht, bidgosht!"

Viki's mother brings us tiny sandwiches that I love more than anything in the world, with cheese and cucumber. "Dziękuję bidgosht!" I say to her and she laughs.

We're sitting on the verandah steps eating the sandwiches. Viki's mother goes inside and comes back out with an atlas like the one my Dad bought me. She opens it and puts her finger, with the pinkest nail polish I've ever seen, on a spot marked in purple.

"This is Poland," she says, "and my father, who is Viki's grandfather, lives there in a city called Bydgoszcz. It's a small city, near a much larger, important one called Gdansk, which is full of big strong workers who build ships."

Viki has big blue eyes like Johnny, my older brother. I once heard my Dad ask my Mum who else in our family has brown eyes like Eddie.

"Rosa the kindergarten teacher!" I piped up.

"Yes," Mum smiled, "Rosa once said to give you cooked fruit when you were suffering from constipation, and she also taught me how to prepare it."

"It's good for the metabolism," I said to Mum. She laughed a lot, holding her tummy.

"Eddie, where do you know that word from?"

I said that Rosa used it, and she also said that in eight years I'll be thirteen and she won't be my kindergarten teacher anymore but that I could visit her at home in St. Kilda and she'd make a celebration called "Bar Mitzvah" which is what they do."

"That's right," Mum said. "Rosa's Jewish."

EDWARD PERKINS
11 April 1961

Johnny, older than I by two years, was inviting me to go out with his friends for my birthday. They were going bowling in the new place in Elizabeth Street in the center of Melbourne, just as Mum came in.

"Eddie, remember when you were little and we lived next door to the Royal Melbourne Hospital where Dad worked?"

Mum pushed a wisp of hair off her face even though none was hanging there. But after she does that movement, all kinds of lectures begin on what needs to be done, or unpleasant news.

"Did something happen to Rosa Cohen?" I ask.

Mum gives me her blue-eyed stare which indicates she's surprised once again how I know what she's about to say.

"Yes, her daughter phoned me." Mum pushed another imaginary wisp of hair off her face. "I'm sorry, Eddie, but Rosa has a brain tumor. She's in the Royal Melbourne and between treatments hasn't stopped asking that Eddie Perkins from her kindergarten come and visit her on his birthday because she promised to celebrate his Bar Mitzvah, and a promise must be kept."

"Tell her," Johnny piped up, "that Eddie will come tomorrow to visit her because today he's coming bowling with us. Isn't that so, Edward Perkins, my li'l bro, who's been in love with his kind teacher since he was four? We're leaving in an hour. I'm taking a quick shower."

I said nothing. It was clear to me that I'd take the tram from South Yarra to the hospital.

Mum smiled at me. "Remember that it's Shabbat today," she said, using the Hebrew word for Sabbath, "and the cafés in St. Kilda will be shut, so eat something before you leave."

A lot of religious Jews populated St. Kilda and closed their businesses on Saturdays, the Shabbat. I thought about Mr. Avraham whose café, "Scheherezade," was on Acland Street. My eyes were always glued to the gray-blue numbers tattooed on his forearm. I could see them when he cut the cake and announced, "Black Forest chocolate cake for the boy with the beautiful eyes" and Mum would smile and say, "Thank you, Mr. Zelnikov," and ask him how his wife Masha was doing.

Once I asked Mum why Mr. Zelnikov had those numbers. "Evil people did that," she said, and I didn't ask about it anymore.

Mum could always understand how my mind worked. She told me that when I was a tiny baby, the place that always calmed my upset tummy the most was next to Dad's vast library. "I'd have to take Johnny for a drive in the car, but the mere scent of those books would calm you, and when I told Rosa she laughed. 'Eddie belongs to the People of the Book,' she'd said, using a phrase often used to describe the Jews.

Three times I passed the room where the nurse said Rosa was lying. I drew closer and saw a diminutive figure. The back of the mattress was raised so that Rosa could sit more comfortably. Around her neck and shoulders were six cushions. I know because I counted them. Two had hospital pillow slips and four had slips in turquoise and green. Her eyes were closed but her lips moved. A sharp pang cut through my stomach. As I turned to go I heard Lily.

"Mum, look who's here?"

"My Eddie," Rosa said without even opening her eyes.

She didn't look like the Rosa I knew, nor like the Rosa I met at Lily's Bat Mitzvah five years ago. Jewish girls often have a coming of age celebration when they turn twelve. Nor did she look like the Rosa I came across at Brighton Beach two years ago. When I was a kindergartener I frequently wondered what color dress Rosa would wear. I loved the turquoise colors the most, and she had plenty of dresses with turquoise in them.

She also wore necklaces made of round or square glass beads in green and turquoise. Sometimes she let me play with them when I stayed longer in kindergarten because Dad was doing surgery at the St. Kilda Hospital and Mum was not yet back from practice with the South Yarra Chamber Ensemble where she played cello.

Her dresses were huge. As she said when she served us soup with kneidlach, which were little dumplings made of ground matzah, "That's the way it is. All my friends thrive on lettuce but I, what can one do, I love kneidlach. And kartoffl. Yes, Eddie, kartoffl is potato. And I especially love katfofflech, little chunks of potato, in the cholent. On Tuesday I'll bring all the children kartoffl from the cholent." Cholent, I knew, was a kind of meat, potato and fava beans stew that religious Jews often cooked before Shabbat and left on a hot plate the whole Shabbat until lunchtime.

"And compote!" I added. Cooked fruit. And Rosa would laugh happily.

All these words would jumble around in my mind and I could literally smell and taste them long before they actually arrived on the table. That must be how paradise smelled, I was sure.

I came closer. When she opened her eyes, I could recognize Rosa. Lily stood and kissed her mother's forehead.

"Mum asked me to step out of the room when you arrived," Lily said.

"How'd she know that I'd come?" "She said that today's your thirteenth birthday and that in kindergarten the two of you had planned that she'd make you a Bar Mitzvah celebration."

I sat down on the chair Lily vacated. Rosa asked me to plump her pillows so she could sit up straighter. She looked at me through her big brown eyes filled with compassion. A gaze familiar from my childhood.

"What are you learning in history?" she asked.

It was the first time Rosa asked the kind of question aunts and uncles would ask as a way of striking up a conversation with a child, but then not listen to the answer. Rosa smiled.

"I don't have much time, and I need to know if you're studying WWII and the Holocaust."

"We studied a bit about that war but more about

WWI and the Battle of Gallipoli in which a lot of soldiers from Australia and New Zealand, the ANZACs, took part."

I was silent for a moment. I knew that I could talk to Rosa about anything without worrying if it was alright, unlike other adults or friends or even Johnny whose faces would show disapproval or discomfort with certain topics.

"What's that word you said? Holocaust?"

"I'm not too well," Rosa said, "but in Jewish tradition a boy, reaching thirteen, reads sections from the Torah, the Bible, to mark this special transitional age. Because I don't have too long left, I need to tell you about what happened to the Jews not so long ago. Really not long before you were born. To describe the situation a word needed to be found. 'Holocaust' is that word."

Even though I'm pretty used to the smells of hospitals because my Dad took me countless times with him to work, I suddenly felt very dizzy. The mix of urine, vomit and medicines was pronounced.

Breathe deep! I said to myself, the way Dad showed me when I was paler than usual after he took me to Royal Melbourne and demonstrated tonsil removals to students on a medical dummy. It was like the surgery I had because of my constant throat infections. Lily came in. I asked her for a glass of water.

"Once you've drunk, open the drawer in the bedside table," Rosa requested.

Three books were inside. "The Rise and Fall of the Third Reich," "The Holocaust of European Jewry," and a book about the Lublin community. I remembered Rosa telling me that her parents came to Australia from a Polish city called Lublin.

"I know you love to read," Rosa said and asked me to read these books about European Jewry and what happened some ten years before I was born. "On this day precisely, your thirteenth birthday, the trial of Adolf Eichmann begins in Jerusalem. He was one of the primary forces behind what the Germans called 'The Final Solution to the Jewish Problem.' Their final solution was to murder six million Jews across Europe. Israel's undercover forces, known as the Mossad, captured Eichmann in Argentina where he had escaped after the war, evading justice under the false name of Ricardo Klement," Rosa explained. Drained of energy, she fell back against the pillows.

She signaled to me to open a little cabinet next to the bed and take out a small radio. Lily had preset the station to let us catch the court hearing which was being broadcast worldwide from Jerusalem. And then I heard a voice that sounded like a hammer being banged against metal.

"When I stand before you here, Judges of Israel, to lead the Prosecution of Adolf Eichmann, I am not standing alone. With me are six million accusers. But they cannot rise to their feet and point an accusing finger towards him who sits in the dock, and cry: "I accuse." For their ashes are piled up on the hills of Auschwitz and the fields of Treblinka, and are strewn in the forests of Poland. Their graves are scattered throughout the length and breadth of Europe. Their blood cries out, but their voice is not heard. Therefore I will be their spokesman and in their name I will unfold the terrible indictment."

We listened for several tense minutes to the trial's opening speech given by Israel's Attorney General, Gideon Hausner.

"Your Bar Mitzvah ceremony is a rite of passage indicating that you have ceased being a child and can now adopt the responsibilities of a man," Rosa said, stroking my cheek as her eyes shone. "Now, please call Lily because I'm feeling a little tired."

She leaned forward to hug me firmly. The scent of eucalyptus oil from my early childhood filled my nostrils, as did the memory of Rosa's cholent. The hospital smells disappeared. I could feel the salty tears in my mouth. I wanted to wipe my face but didn't move. A week later, Rosa Cohen passed away.

Every year on my birthday for years afterwards Johnny asks if it had really been worth foregoing the bowling party for the Bar Mitzvah that my kindergarten teacher Rosa provided.

I never answer.

TALYA KARLINSKI
20 April 1964

Before the activity marking Yom HaShoah, as Holocaust Day is called in Israel, the group guide Amiram wished me a happy birthday.

"Our Talya, who is passionate about literature and theater and has a poem ready for every event, is only sixteen but I have no doubt that one day we'll be walking into bookstores and seeing a book by Talya Karlinski on the shelves. Nor will she change her name or alter it when she marries, so watch out for that book! This time she insists on a poem by Shlonski, which we'll read in our meeting."

Everyone was enjoying the chocolate cake that Rona and I baked using her grandmother's recipe. Rona had been raised by her grandmother after her mother died when she was in 8th grade. Rona hugged me super tight the way she did every time she could tell by my eyes welling up that a stomach-ache was beginning.

In kindergarten, our teacher Tsipporah told us that she has a number tattooed on her forearm because the Germans, "may their names and memories be forever erased," she always added, did that to her. In 1st grade our teacher Rina asked us to draw pictures that connect to the words "six million, crematoria, and concentration camps." In Grade 2, Rina asked us to write sentences using those very same words. When we were in the 3rd grade, Rina asked us to write a short composition using those words and an additional word: Shoah.

I was sixteen when Rona sat next to me and read "I dreamt a very terrible dream," and it was the first time that, instead of seeing "I have no people, they are no more," the image of a little boy with huge brown, lightly hooded eyes ringed by long eyelashes came up in my mind. His left cheek was dimpled, and an angelic smile lit his face. It was as angelic as the images I saw in the artist Raphael's paintings on our trip to the Vatican.

"Talya, what's up with you?" I heard Rona's voice. "You're shaking."

"I have to go home. I need Herman to tell me exactly how Yosseleh was murdered," I whispered.

"*Yosseleh meineh yingeleh, Yosseleh meineh sheyneh ponom, Yosseleh meineh kind!*" Herman would shout these Yiddish phrases in his sleep: Yosseleh my boy, my sweet faced Yosseleh, Yosseleh my boy. And I'd cringe in bed, wanting to become the little ladybug without ears. In the morning all I wanted was to be Talya who goes to school and sings "When spring flowers blossom we will stroll through the meadow."

"But we're in the middle of the activity!" Rona said through almost closed lips.

Nonetheless, I stood, left the room, raced outside and flung myself onto my bike, riding home as fast as I could. On the way, I swore I wouldn't interrupt the story. I'd let Herman speak the way he told me stories when I was little and he'd arrange the feather pillows, sit me on them, and tell me about Yosseleh who was his sister Hava's son, a chess champion, and a beautiful child, as well as incredibly smart and well-mannered.

Up until I was six, I'd listen to every word, but I remember how my attentiveness lessened once our teacher Rina asked us to compose sentences. Slowly Herman stopped talking about Yosseleh and the fact that he never managed to get back and save the family. Abba also stopped singing me lullabies, especially the one about the little boy who closed his big dark eyes.

"Our literature loving Talya is switching to history," Rona told her friend. "She asked Hirshbein, our history teacher, if she could do a project about the destruction of the Jews of Lublin. It's not even related to the matriculation material."

"Well, there are students who research biology, such as isotopes. So I'm doing research too," I said. I had a special relationship with Dr. Hirshbein, who was also our home teacher.

"I'm in favor but I want facts, facts, facts," Dr. Hirshbein agreed in his heavy Polish accent. People said he was a Shoah survivor from Krakow. People said he was from the Płaszów forced labor camp, and that its sadistic commander, Amon Leopold Göth, loved how he played the violin so kept him alive.

Once, in a home school class when we discussing our study plans after our final exams and military service, Hirshbein told us he'd been privileged to teach history at the Krakow Jagiellonian University, one of the oldest in all "Eroppa." He never pronounced it "Europe." Copernicus had been among the graduates of that illustrious academic institution. Then there was a long silence, then he coughed, sat on a chair, and Rona raced out to bring him a glass of water. Right then the bell rang for the end of class.

"Best of luck, Talya," he smiled at me.

I read piles of material. I quickly familiarized with the name of Herman Worthoff, the Lublin Region Commander who personally shot Dr. Mark Altan, chairman of the Judenrat, during the Lublin ghetto's extermination. I also learned about Shammai Greier, apparently a kind of Jewish Gestapo agent who served the best quality alcohol to Gestapo officers while the Jewish orchestra played background music in his Lobartowska Street restaurant. Greier was sure that by cozying up to the Gestapo he would be safe from their evil. He also shot Monjek Goldfarb, the commander of the ghetto's Jewish police force.

Over and over again, a certain name kept appearing on the documents: a particularly nasty SS officer named Ludwig Schmidt, who was Worthoff's deputy. Schmidt was passionate about chess, and about chamber quartets which he took with him everywhere in the ghetto. When I ask Dr. Hirshbein if there's some connection, in his view, between Schmidt and Yosseleh, who was a chess maestro, his answer is clipped.

"Only facts, my young Miss Karlinski."

SOPHIE SCHMIDT
1 September 1965

On my sixteenth birthday, I discovered I'm the daughter of a murderer. An hour before that birthday and the party I was planning for my best friends, I happened to go down into the basement to look for some fancy dress costumes. I remembered once seeing all kinds of old clothes on metal hangers: ball gowns, black suits, gray suits, masks with big noses, masks with red horns.

"Sophie, I'm going to the grocer's. I'm out of sugar for the gingerbread," I heard Mama say.

Great! No one will disturb me! That was my first thought. She and Papa were always saying there was no reason for me to go into the basement. I'd find nothing but mice, dirt and bacteria.

"And you're my little one-and-only princess," Papa would smile at me, "who needs not only to be pretty and smart but also healthy."

"My Papa isn't like all the other fathers in Heidelberg," I told Frau Schultz, my Grade 1 teacher. "Almost every day in the afternoon he teaches me a game called chess. He says that only clever people play it."

By the time I was five, I realized that everyone, from my teachers and friends, neighbors and the grocer, to the city clerk, my cousins Karl and Mattheus, everyone, loved my Papa. They said I'm so lucky that I was born to Ludwig and Marta Schmidt.

I opened the large black chest, lifted a photo album out, and began leafing through it. There is my Papa, Ludwig, standing with his legs slightly apart, in a uniform and a black hat with a skull on it. The SS emblem. There's Ludwig and Marta hugging each other in a boat on the river, surrounded by happily laughing friends, all of them in uniform. There's Ludwig with a whip in hand standing over a man, bent over. Dozens of photos.

Among them, one stood out: Ludwig and a skinny lad whose eyes are adorned by thick long eyelashes. Those eyes shine like gold and fire. They're sitting at a table in a place that looks like a military camp. Both have their chins resting on their right palms, and they're deep in thought. In front of them is the chess board. Ludwig wears a fur coat over his uniform. The skinny youth wears a shirt under a sweater that doesn't look especially warm. Turning the photo over, I see the date: November 1942.

I keep rummaging through the box and find love letters to Marta where Papa details how he'll hug and kiss every bit of her body when they get together. Reaching to the chest's base, my fingers touch a cold, hard metallic object. It's the black whip, smelling as strong as though it had just been in use.

I sit down on a chair because my head is spinning. I see the basement, the spiders' webs, the costumes, mice nibbling on things. Everything flashes by at the speed of light. Closing my eyes tight, I think: I must not get sick,

I must not faint, I must stay focused, I've got to function. I have to decide what to do. Uncle Heinrich, who's a doctor, recommended to Mama once when she felt dizzy that she should lie on the floor and raise her legs.

So I lie down. I want to scream: how stupid could I possibly have been? All these stories that he'd been a soldier, wounded, barely involved in the war: what a convenient version of events. Frau Eisenberg spoke in class about the Auschwitz Trials held in Frankfurt because the Hessen Attorney General, Franz Bauer, insisted that the death factories operating in Germany and elsewhere should be disclosed to the German public. After that, I asked Papa again where he'd been during the war.

"Princess," he reassured in a firm voice, "there was a war, I served, I was wounded in August 1941, and after my recovery was sent as adjutant to the regional commander in Poland. I was an office clerk."

"What was the commander's name?"

"Herman Worthoff."

Papa knew how much I loved to investigate and learn the details of any story I heard, and so he provided them right away. Then he hugged me. It was the familiar smell of my Papa.

I was half awake when I heard the door slam and Mama calling out.

"Sophie, where are you? I brought the sugar."

Get up very slowly, I instructed myself in my uncle's voice.

When my friends showed up for the birthday party, Mama had no choice but to tell them it had been postponed because I was feverish. But by then I wasn't home. I remember the last time I'd spoken to Frau Eisenberg, my beloved history teacher, before she was fired. Rumor had it that she was Jewish and teaching incorrect versions of our history. Our teachers kept explaining and writing figures and information on the blackboard. Their eyes shone, some of them even had froth at the corners of their mouths when they spoke excitedly of how the German people had fallen victim to the Nazi regime. But Frau Eisenberg claimed, in her soft, confident voice, that the bulk of Germany's population cooperated with the Nazis, and many deeply admired Hitler.

Before she left, Frau Eisenberg called me over. "Of all my students, I would ask of you, my dear Sophie, to remember Fritz Bauer's words: 'We cannot create a paradise on earth, but each of us can do something so that this earth will not become a hell.' I'm moving to Berlin," she smiled, slipping a note with her new address into my hand.

2 September 1965

On opening her door and seeing me, Frau Eisenberg smiled warmly. She lived with Carolina, her tabby, in a tiny apartment next to the zoo.

"Sophie, my dear! You remembered to visit. Which hotel are your parents in?" She glanced down for a moment. "And why are you lugging such a large bag around?"

Before I had time to answer I could tell from her eyes and the way she squeezed her lips tight, familiar from our history classes when someone asked a question that had no simple, unequivocal answer, that she understood.

"Come in, come in. You must be tired, Sophie."

"You must know that my father is a stinking murderer and that all these years he lied to me," I blurted, "and I'm not going back to my Nazi parents, nor am I part of the German people."

I sat down on my teacher's sofa. She served me hot tea and a slice of Kaiser roll spread with butter and raspberry jam.

"You know, I loved my name, because I knew that Papa chose it for me. It has a gentle, caressing sound. 'Repeat after me,' he'd tell me, whispering it when he finished reading 'Rumpelstiltskin' to me at bedtime. 'Sophie, my lovely Sophie, good night and sweet dreams.' Sometimes when he was angry because I didn't take my boots off at the front door but walked into the house with mud on them, or forgot to take our Labrador Leopold for a walk even though I promised to look after him as a condition for Papa buying me the dog, he'd peek over the top of his newspaper. 'Sophie Schmidt, Sophie Schmidt,' was all he said, and I immediately went to fix up what I'd done wrong."

Drawing in a breath, I raced on. "When my uncles would get together for Christmas or Mama's birthday or for a concert organized by Aunt Louisa and Uncle Heinrich, who is Papa's brother, they'd clink their crystal glasses together. 'Speech, Ludwig, speech!' they'd shout, because everyone loved his rich deep voice."

I barely caught my breath. "Stinking Nazi."

I couldn't stop talking. Frau Eisenberg stroked my hair and said sweet, kind words. But I plowed on, the words spilling in a rush, my pulse banging in my temples.

Suddenly I felt a pillow being gently pushed under my head, and a blanket being spread over me, and my forehead and hair softly stroked, but I mumbled on, unable to stop until at last the world around me faded away. From a very great distance I heard Frau Eisenberg's voice. She must've been talking on the phone.

Sleep was welcome.

The phone didn't stop ringing. I could hear it as I dozed and woke, dozed and woke.

"Frau Schmidt, there's no need to cry. It's typical of teenage moods, rebelling against parents. She'll come back. She's in good hands. I'm looking after her well."

And then: "Yes, Herr Schmidt, I understand. I understand. Yes, I realize that a very different story can be put together from photos alone."

"Yes, I understand."

"Yes, Sophie's very dear to me. She's a single child. You went through so much. You didn't support the Nazi party."

"Ah, of course, you were forced to enlist."

"Yes, no more than a soldier."

"She's asleep now. I'll ask her to call you."

EDWARD
The University of Sydney, 1966

"Nice to meet you. I'm Karl," the student sitting next to me in the Prince Alfred Hall at the Royal Hospital introduced himself in our preliminary class on the anatomy of the brain.

His eyes were almost bluer than those of my brother, Johnny.

"Edward," I said, "but I'm okay with Eddie."

After class we went for a beer at a pub in Darlinghurst.

"Even though the pub's called 'Chamberlain' they serve the best beer in all Sydney."

"Neville Chamberlain?" Karl asked, grinning. His understanding smile made me warm to him right away.

"What's so special about Darlinghurst? Friends recommended the neighborhood instead of the dorms. I'm here from Heidelberg for one year on an exchange student program. I definitely need guidance on Sydney's mysteries," Karl said.

"Well, from today on consider yourself part of the Perkins family. My Mum's an expert in adopting mine and my brother Johnny's friends. You actually look a bit like him with those sea colored eyes and wheat colored hair, which is how Mum describes him. As for Darlinghurst, it's got great book stores, gyms, incredible organic food shops and cafés, and it's become the cultural and residential center for Sydney's homosexual community."

Every Monday afternoon in the Churchill Hall the university chess club holds competitions. Karl loves joining me.

"You wipe them all out!" he laughs.

He doesn't play but told me that his uncle Ludwig said playing chess helped him survive the war.

"Well, the main thing is, you're with us," he'd say to his uncle who, with his wife Marta, would nod and laugh raucously.

"What do you mean, 'survive?'" I ask Karl, "because so far I've only ever heard that word used relative to Jews who survived the Holocaust."

"True," Karl said. "The first time I noticed that word was when Ludwig said it was problematic after I mentioned our teacher using it in history class in Heidelberg. Frau Eisenberg, the teacher, showed us films about the extermination of Jews in the Holocaust, and used the word 'survive' for those who, well, became survivors. When we were in 11th grade she was allowed to take us on a history trip by train to Frankfurt, and basically led us to the district court where we watched the Auschwitz Trials convening. As preparation, she told us about Fritz Bauer, the Hessen AG who initiated putting those in charge of the Auschwitz Extermination Camp on trial."

Karl halted for a moment. "Of course once the school management discovered what our trip was about, and that it wasn't a regular history trip at all, Frau Eisenberg was fired. But afterwards I spent a lot of time reading and studying the Holocaust on my own," Karl explained. "So, wow, I can't believe I just actually said 'survive' vis-à-vis my uncle."

We're on our way to a chess competition in the building next door to the Royal Hospital. This is the final stage of the State of New South Wales Chess Tournament.

And this conversation with Karl isn't helping me as the game approaches. I try to stay focused. And anyhow, why does he need to come with me to every game? I wonder. I can hear my Mum Beth's voice rebuking Johnny after she heard him talking to one of his friends rather gruffly.

"Rudeness to a friend is not acceptable in the Perkins family."

Rosa flashes into my thoughts, smiling, in her big, turquoise dress. Then her image gently fades into a tiny body telling me to listen to Karl more closely. Gidon Hausner's metallic voice rings in my ears. I drop down onto the green bench at the hall's entrance.

"What's up? Karl asks.

"My concentration went out the window," I say.

"But you've got an amazing brain, so just command it to refocus."

I know exactly what he's thinking: Eddie's Jewish, has typically big brown eyes, surrounded by long lashes, and his mind is not focused.

But I'm crazy about the game, and there's my ambition to win. Every time.

In Karl's mind, on the other hand, very different thoughts are spinning: We could sit here on the bench, and I could tell Eddie about Sophie, my cousin, Karl thinks. Ludwig's daughter. The uncle who said that chess saved him in the war.

Instead of hurrying off to the competition, I stay on the bench. I can feel weakness in my legs and shoulders. My mouth is dry. I think of the Bar Mitzvah "party" in hospital with Rosa. Closing my eyes, I can hear Karl's voice.

"Sophie and I grew up like brother and sister. She's only a year younger than me. On her sixteenth birthday, she went into the family's basement. She wanted some fancy dress gear for friends coming to her birthday party. For the first time in her life she opened the big black chest that had always stood there, and found photos of her father, Ludwig, standing proudly in his SS uniform. She also found a black whip that smelled as strong as though it had just been used the day before. Piles of letters from Ludwig to Marta, his wife, from when he was in Poland, and how thrilled he was to be going home to Heidelberg for the Easter vacation."
"Marta came back from shopping for the party, but Sophie was already at the train station. All she had was her history teacher's new address in Berlin. Sophie and I write to each other. She's finishing high school in Berlin now."

I ball my fists and stuff them in my pockets as a way of making sure I don't smash Karl Schmidt in the face. I've missed the chess final!

Standing, without looking back, I walk quickly away.

SOPHIE SCHMIDT
4 September 1965

Of one thing I'm absolutely certain: I'm never going back to Heidelberg. I won't study in a school that hides history, just like that man in the photo hides history. He played chess every day with the scarecrow-thin kid in the big loose sweater, that man who says he was forced to enlist, was a regular soldier, and was later wounded.

Now I know that he's hiding a dark secret.

A murderer's secret.

A murderer of children.

Ludwig. The man I used to call Papa. And who I will never call Papa again.

It used to be that mothers and children who recognized me in shops would say, "How lucky you are, Sophie, to have Ludwig as your father. He's not like other fathers. He doesn't get angry or shout at children when they make a noise. He just gently asks if they can be a bit quieter, and he always smiles apologetically, as though he's the one who doesn't want to disturb their games. Nor does he raise his voice in parent-teacher meetings, and is always ready to help on outings and events and festivities we celebrate at school."

Frau Eisenberg teaches at the Jewish school not far from her home near the zoo. There's a metro station nearby of the same name. I want to finish high school where she teaches.

Ludwig screeches into the phone. "But she's a minor. She has to return home."

I can hear Frau Eisenberg speaking calmly. "Well, here, let's call her to the phone."

And I know that Ludwig understands there's no way I'll talk to him, and that even if he got me back home, I'd just run away again. It looks like Ludwig and Marta, which is how I'm going to refer to them from now on, have figured I'm never going back to Heidelberg and threats won't help.

In my mind I can see him removing his glasses, their lenses fogged up, and his face is bright red. I keep thinking about the boy in the photo who must surely have heard Ludwig's screechy voice if he made a mistake on the chessboard, or if the boots he probably had to polish for Ludwig weren't shiny enough. Maybe Ludwig even cracked the whip over him.

I fall into a deep sleep, then suddenly wake in terror and feel a hand on my hair or face. Drifting in and out of sleep, I hear whispers.

"Yes, she'll be alright, don't worry. She needs plenty of rest after that psychological shock, especially having made the discovery as an adolescent."

"Thank you, doctor."

Every food she makes in this tranquil house is tasty: tea with a slice of lemon gently folded over, a piece of herring, a pickled gherkin. I wonder how long she'll continue letting me stay in her house. But I fall back into that deep sleep I've only experienced ever since exploring the basement.

Precisely on the day when I decided I can't be a bother to her anymore, as I was coming out of the shower, she called me over.

"Sophie, we need to have a talk."

I was scared to death that she'd say I'm a minor and must return to Heidelberg. I stared at her gentle hands resting on the table. I remembered that after the 7th Grade Parents Day, I heard Marta telling our neighbor Ingrid who came over for coffee all kinds of details about my history teacher, who married one week before November 11th, 1938, to the son of the family which owned the largest general store in Heidelberg, the famous Eisenberg Centrum. A huge sign hung outside said, "Everything You Need You Can Find Here."

Then I remember Marta's and Ingrid's voices dropping to barely a whisper when they saw me coming, but I heard snippets. "They burnt the store down," "a nice looking young man," "young widow," "Dachau." I took a Kaiser roll spread with cherry jam, smiled at Ingrid, asked politely how she was, and went back to my room to finish my history homework.

Her hands have no rings.

Ever since losing her young, handsome, wealthy husband, I realize, she's been alone.

"Ancestors sin and the descendants end up paying for it," she was saying to me, but I kept thinking: she survived. "We don't choose our parents. We can't be responsible for their actions. The irony is that throughout the generations, the children suffer because of their parents' actions. Do you understand that, Sophie?"

That's what her gentle voice said. And my tears began to flow. For the first time since smelling the whip in the Schmidt's basement, I cried.

"I'm stupid. So stupid. All the signs were there," I sobbed.

She held me in a warm embrace. "Sophie, dear, you're experiencing a crisis. You've discovered a very harsh truth about the people closest to you. But you're sixteen, and so we must receive your parents' permission before we do anything. They're still your parents, they love you, and are concerned about you."

Between bursts of tears I hear her repeat these words. The lump in my throat begins to dissolve. Frau Eisenberg will help me, I think, because she said 'we.' She tells me that she's already spoken to them about the possibility of allowing me to stay with her and finish my studies in the Berlin high school.

"Ludwig will receive reports from me on your progress, and for the moment this looks like the best option until you agree to meet them and talk with them. They do love you, Sophie, and they're worried about you," she says again, but her tone is flat and factual rather than emotional, which makes things easier for me because I don't feel she's pressuring me into anything.

"They do wish to meet you, though," she says, almost in a whisper.

Emphatically I shake my head the way I did every time she presented Ludwig's and Marta's request during that week of sleeping and waking when my thoughts were racing not in my mind, but up and down my body, all the way from the roots of my hair to my little toe. I kept imagining how I'd kill myself because I didn't have a reason to live with two murderers. If I killed myself, I'd sever our murderous lineage. The verdict was in: I was not only an exemplar of that satanic race of Aryans, I was also the daughter of a murderer and a murderer's accomplice.

I lay down across the bed, feeling my bare feet hanging out in the air. Who's really to blame? Where could a finger be pointed? Only at Ludwig and Marta? Then I remembered Karl, my cousin, son of my uncle Dr. Heinrich. I love Karl. Whenever we talked he'd say "Sophie, try to be more precise in formulating your thoughts."

That was the day I got up from my bed.

"Aaah," Frau Eisenberg strokes my wet hair, "you used the herbal shampoo I bought you. Wunderbar!" she adds, as she smiles warmly. Wonderful!

"I'm going to write a letter to my cousin Karl today. He's like my brother. He went to Australia to study."

"Also wunderbar!" Frau Eisenberg smiles again.

I see that Sarah Eisenberg is noting my improved mood and is very pleased. I hug her tight, too.

EDWARD
15 June 1967

"Now's the best time to go to Israel," Karl says.

I look up from the brain anatomy book I was studying. How does this guy from Heidelberg manage to hook up with my most secret thoughts?

There, at the furthest end of the world, a war had just taken place. There, survivors and their children who'd witnessed the Eichmann Trials had just won against enemies who rose up against them. Ever since the bar mitzvah that Rosa marked, the thought of that hell in Europe pierces my heart every day. It may take no more than a fraction of a second, a flash, sometimes a little longer. I've become accustomed to living with it. A secret dialogue between me and my brain.

"Go to Israel…" I repeat.

"Well, I'm going to visit my cousin Sophie. She moved there right after finishing high school in Berlin. Frau Eisenberg contacted the Jewish Agency offices in Berlin and arranged for her to join a kibbutz in the north, near Haifa. I can't imagine you've forgotten the story I told you about Sophie, who fled her home after discovering what her father Ludwig had done, right?"

"Yes, you told me on the day I ended up missing the

chess tournament. That story completely broke my focus, and I'm not sure I'll ever forgive you," I laugh.

"In her latest letter, she writes 'Bring Eddie, they really need a lot of friends here to help because most of the men are still recruited in military service.'"

"Yes, I read about how Israel really needs volunteers from all over the world, especially for agriculture," I say, but inside my brain there's a buzz, an instruction, a list of sorts:

Read up on Rosa's ancestral land.
Visit the place where the Eichmann Trials were held.
Go to Israel.

I went home for the weekend. Mum was practicing St. Saens' cello movement called "The Swan" for the festive recital which would open the National Academy of Music in South Melbourne's Bank Street. Sitting on a green chair, I listen closely. She smiles the same way she did on the first day she left me somewhere new and unfamiliar, my first day at Rosa's kindergarten. I was on the verge of tears but her message to me was clear and firm: "Eddie, everything will be fine here, and when you're ready to say bye-bye, Mummy will go off for a little bit, and always come back."

"How are you, Eddie?" she asks, putting the cello delicately into its stand.

I hug the cellist Beth Perkins and give her a book of poems which I found in Roger's used books store in Darlinghurst.

"My beloved Yeats," she flips the book open and reads:
"I know that I shall meet my fate
Somewhere among the clouds above;

Those that I fight I do not hate,
Those that I guard I do not love;"

"How come you opened the book at 'An Irish Airman Foresees His Death?'"

Mum laughs. I continue.

"A waste of breath the years behind
In balance with this life, this death."

Those are the closing lines of the poem Mum always quoted whenever a war made the headlines, including the Six Day War two weeks earlier in the Middle East.

"Maybe it wasn't chance that you opened the book at that poem," I suggest. "I'm thinking of taking a year off from my studies and going with Karl to volunteer in Israel. But don't worry, I'll come back. You know how important my medical studies are to me."

Mum's pretty face blushed hard. It was one of the few times in my life that I sensed my mother was furious with me. But she never said a word. Instead, she lifted the cello out of its holder, put it in its case, closed the clips, and went to Dad's work room. I could hear them conversing in hushed tones. She was upset, but I knew he'd calm her.

Before my return to Sydney, she hugged me.

"I do have a request," she said. "Please come and spend a few days with us before you fly overseas."

TALYA KARLINSKI:
16 September 1967

Abba was buried today in the kibbutz cemetery. Even though it was September, which is usually hot and dry, it never stopped raining. Drops fell on that large body, that blue-eyed man, who always wore a tailored suit even when he was sitting at the radio intently listening to the Search for Relatives program.

Even though I was little, with ribbons tied around my braids and little sailor-collared tops, and even though I really wanted him to bounce me up and down on his lap like he always did when I came back from school, or after playing hopscotch with Naomi, or climbing the berry tree, I knew that when the Search for Relatives program was on, I must never disturb him. But I did see the tears rolling down his beautiful face, and his blue eyes shining even more.

I brought Abba for burial in the kibbutz.

Noah phoned Base 80 and organized my release from cadet training to attend the funeral.

"Don't worry" he said, "I'll handle all the arrangements."

He made sure that the body was brought from Ichilov Hospital in Tel Aviv to the kibbutz. In a phone call he asked me to add my mother's name to the notices of death that the kibbutz would be publishing in the papers.

"No. If she wants to be here for the week of mourning, let her publish her own notices in America, if she can even find the time between her shows on Broadway, the Guggenheim Museum and dinners with her brand new, rich husband."

"Talya, sweetie," Noah said in his vibrant deep voice, "it's all arranged, and I know you'll be here soon. Sophie will wait for you at the kibbutz bus stop. The funeral will be very respectable, don't worry."

Suddenly I felt the tears climbing up my throat. Three days ago when I visited Abba in the oncology department, he'd looked so wasted. His hair had been combed with the parting on the right. There he sat, propped up by pillows, and began talking about Yosseleh, his nephew, his sister's son, the same Yosseleh he'd told me about when I was a little girl.

"You know, I'm sure that if Yossi had a grave and you asked him what name to carve into the headstone, he'd have said 'Yossef Karlinski.' He'd have taken his mother Hava's family name, and that of his Zeideh, Rabbi Karlinski. He was so attached to them."

Abba paused before continuing. "I want to ask you, Talya, not to give up the name Karlinski. Not ever. I'm sure whoever your future husband is won't oppose you keeping the name. After I'm gone, you'll be the only person alive with that name."

Never before had my Abba, Herman Karlinski, spoken to me about the importance of our family name.

"Did I ever tell you what the name Herman means?" he asked suddenly, I was on my way to bring him strong tea with lemon in the delicate glass I'd brought from home. I spun back to face him.

"No, Abba, we've never spoken about the name's meaning. But I do remember asking you why you had so many names and you said that each of them helped save you when you fled the Nazis. And then I said that instead of calling you Abba like all kids say when they mean their fathers, I'll also call you Herman. Remember?"

That special smile that I loved so much was sent my way. I sat down on the chair next to him.

"Herman is a German name. My mother loved German culture. She studied German and could speak it well. In her youth she traveled with her parents to Germany and fell in love with the poetry of Heine and Goethe, so much so that she had a shelf in the bookcase filled with German books. She told me that when my father wanted to name me Simha, in honor of the renowned Rabbi Simha Bunim of Przysucha, she said that there were enough Hassids with that name already."

Abba smiled at me. "Yes. My mother had a sense of humor typical of a wealthy family which felt part of the Polish intellectual class. When I was sixteen I asked her if I could stop sharing a room with my younger brother because I needed my privacy. 'Heniek,' she said to me. That was the Polish way of saying Herman that we used at home. 'Heniek, I've been waiting for this request, because your name is one that is shared by others who have a spiritual or philosophical nature, and need their peace of mind and a quiet spot. Very intelligent people. Introverted people. And that's what you are, so I'll make sure you have a place of your own.'"

"I remember hugging her. I knew she had a large book listing German names where she'd probably read about the name she chose for her firstborn son."

And there was Abba's smile again.

"I'll see you next week," I said, kissing his forehead.

"Yes, my lovely girl." And his blue eyes shone.

Those were the last words I heard him speak.

TALYA KARLINSKI:
30 September 1967

"It's been two weeks since your Abba's funeral," Sophie says to me. "You're just sitting at home not doing a thing. You need to get out. Noah's organizing a bonfire to celebrate the successful banana harvest."

"Sophie, his words echo in my thoughts. 'Keep the name Karlinski. After I go the name will disappear.' Never in all the stories of his murdered family by those Goethe lovers, and his stories about Yosseleh, did he ever emphasize the importance of our family name."

"Come here," Sophie said softly holding her arms open to me. Like a rag doll, I flopped into them, the tears which had disappeared after the funeral flooding back.

"Shake yourself up a bit with us. We all love you so much. My cousin Karl's friend Eddie will also be there. Karl says you remind him of Eddie, actually: sort of philosophical, serious, yet funny, and you won't believe it but he's also addicted to chess!"

Sophie's already at the door, smiling, blowing me a kiss. "Please, please come. I'm sure Abba Herman would agree it's good for you and even encourage you."

Sophie is one of those people who always has a hug

ready when it's needed but doesn't waste time on excess or unnecessary emotion.

When Abba first saw her the first question he asked, using the Yiddish for a non-Jewish woman, was: "Who's that shikseh?"

"Sshh," I whispered, "she's a good friend, a volunteer from Germany."

Sophie, her mane of blond curls, and her brilliant smile, came towards us from the other side of Kibbutz Ein Yam's dining hall. It was where we stayed during our pre-military recruit training. She held her hand out to Abba.

"I'm so glad to meet you at last, Mr. Karlinski."

Abba smiled. "Well, while it's true that we're both from Eroppa, here the custom is first names. So please, call me Herman."

"A not unfamiliar name," Sophie smiled back.

Sophie and Abba clicked immediately. I loved hearing her enunciate his name perfectly. Of course he invited her to sit with us for lunch but first he stood and helped her ease out of her coat, then pull a chair out for her. I hear them laughing as I return to the table with glasses of soda.

"Herman agrees with me that because you're so deeply in thought you sometimes forget to enjoy yourself and laugh."

"Hirshbein, my history teacher, who really liked me, removed me from class twice for bursting into laughter and disrupting my serious friend Rona's seriousness!"

"Well, of course if you're going to compare yourself to Rona…" Sophie broke into laughter.

After the customary week-long mourning period I spent my days in a beloved faded pajama. For hours I sat on the floor among piles of documents that I'd brought from Abba's former Tel Aviv home in Gruzenberg Street, bawling my eyes out.

My parents' divorce papers.

Letters Abba wrote to the Search for Relatives department at the radio station, and to various government bodies, seeking his lost siblings.

"Yosseleh was most certainly murdered because he was taken with my sister to the ghetto, but perhaps my brother Yidl survived because he was in the Red Army," he said, but although he was speaking to me, he sounded more like he was talking to himself. These kinds of things would get mentioned as he tucked me into bed.

Among the documents I found three letters from a woman named Christina. They were in Polish and from Lublin. I slipped them into the brown leather bag Abba had stitched for me, telling myself that one day I'd try to unravel the letters' contents.

I have to get outside to breathe. Sophie's right: the time has come.

A white buttoned top, blue pants. The simplest clothes: that's what I'd wear, I decided. Definitely suitable for a bonfire.

I could hear his voice. Something about it was familiar. But how could it be familiar? After all, we'd never met.

He's from Australia. Speaks English. Scattered words of Hebrew.

Jeans and a black polo shirt.

I can see his profile. Talking to Sophie. Tall. Slim.

I can feel my pulse pounding in my temples.

I sing "Tell me, doe of love, why you covered your head with a violet shawl."

Instead of bursting into tears I laugh out loud as I pretend to listen to Noah telling us about terrorists discovered as they waited in ambush on the banks of the Jordan River after the war.

"You must've been dreaming," I say. You must never let Noah know you aren't interested in his stories.

"Talya, someone would like to meet you.."

Now I can see his face in the bonfire's light. Large brown eyes, with a dreamlike gaze. Not penetrating but not avoiding. He holds his hand out: his fingers are long, as though sculpted.

"Nice to meet you. Edward Perkins, but everyone calls me Eddie." His smile is hesitant.

"You have a pianist's hands," I blurt, surprising even myself. Then I laugh uncontrollably.

"This is our Talya," Sophie says, her hand on my shoulder.

EDWARD PERKINS:
September 1967

"Lower the hand of bananas really gently on the tractor's wagon," Sophie's friend Noah shouts. He's back from a week of reserve duty and already organizing recruitment for the continued banana harvest. He told me that his unit was involved in cleaning up ambushes along the Jordan River's banks, looking for terrorists planning actions inside Israel, when suddenly through his binoculars he noticed the strap of a water canteen slung over the border fence.

"I called the platoon commander and he sent me to lead our unit out to catch them. We caught the terrorists and brought them into the command center. When I told the guys that we'd picked up terrorists who'd crossed the river, they said I must be hallucinating. But I was right," he said, thumping me on the shoulder that was hurting after loading so many bananas, grinning from ear to ear, his bright white teeth flashing in his freckled face.

"Madhim," I said.

"Your Hebrew's improved a lot. 'Madhim' instead of amazing, huh?" he laughed. "After this we're going down to the beach. I hope Talya's back from her week of mourning for her father and she'll join us. She's really into the same world of chess as you."

Before I saw her face, I heard her laughter. Then I heard her voice when everyone sang "Tell me, doe of love, why you covered your head with a violet shawl." Afterwards, in the bonfire's light, I saw her profile: although it was hard to tell the color, she had large eyes ringed in thick lashes, a pug nose, and a small mouth.

A brown beauty spot on her cheek.

Hair that cascaded down to her waist.

Edward Perkins, I thought, this is a moment you'll remember all your life.

You'll write a poem about it.

I'm putting a list together in my mind:
Talk slowly, so your voice doesn't jump to a higher octave the way it does when you get excited;
Don't talk too much;
Don't stay too quiet;
Don't be afraid to talk in Hebrew;
Don't be afraid to switch to English;
Don't apologize all the time;
Stay cool.

Sophie's saying "Eddie, come here, I'd like you to meet a friend I love, Talya."

I move closer to the bonfire. Talya's standing. Blue pants, white cotton top with buttons, the kind that my mum has plenty of. On her right hand's middle finger she's wearing a large ring set with a turquoise.

She holds her hand out towards me. That ring.

"Nice to meet you," she says.

"Na'im me'od."

I say the same, but in Hebrew. Now I can see not just her profile. What a shame Karl's gone back to recommence his studies in Ruprecht. He'd have said I should ask her to walk with me on the beach, tell her about Melbourne's Tram Line 57 which I took to visit my kindergarten teacher, Rosa. Just don't tell her about Rosa's cancer. Don't talk about the Eichmann Trials. Don't tell her about classes in brain anatomy. Don't tell her too many things. Let her do the talking. She's just lost her father, who had brain cancer, and Sophie says she was very close to him.

And also, don't pay any attention to her seeming to laugh a lot. It's her release, instead of crying.

SOPHIE SCHMIDT
6 September 1970

Talya insisted on trying the dress on so Eddie would see it. Our custom was that the groom doesn't see the bride's dress. But "our custo'm" doesn't really hold in kibbutz. After all, I'm living with Noah in Kibbutz Ein Yam. That's "our custom" for me now.

My stomach's churning as I wait for Talya to show up for her makeup. Very light, as she requested. And have her hair done the way she wanted it. "Your wild ponytail has to be nicely done for the wedding, and I'll make sure of that," I told her before I flew back for Ludwig's funeral.

"Take my hair dryer," Mama said with an apologetic smile. "I'm sure you don't have such good ones there. it will help get your friend Talya ready for her wedding. Karl told me how important it was for you to be there, especially since you're her bridesmaid."

I never agreed to meet my father Ludwig from the day I left my parents' house. I did eventually agree to meet Mama before leaving Berlin.

"You won't be able to commence your new life in Israel as a clean slate without making your farewells from your Mama, especially since you say you do still have some good childhood memories. It's important that at least when it comes to Marta, you close the circle in some way, my dear Sophie," Mrs. Eisenberg had said, tears welling in her eyes.

Mrs. Eisenberg: this woman I loved, admired, who provided me with a warm home, who saved my soul during the two years I spent in Berlin.

"Don't worry. I'll meet with Marta," I said.

And I did, one day before I left Berlin together with Noah. We sat at a café near the zoo. I sought the right words. My mother was gazing at my face, trying to read my emotions, my thoughts. So I tried to look severe.

She took my hand in hers. In a hoarse, shaking voice, she spoke. "I'm so proud of you for completing your studies with honors despite the crisis you went through."

And at that moment I burst into tears.

Now my eyes are dry.

We have just buried my father, who until I was sixteen was the person I loved the most, the most significant person in my life.

"While he was still conscious he asked me to tell you how sorry he was, and that nevertheless he loved you so much."

That harsh visage which I artificially adopted when bidding my mother farewell became the true, deep way I related internally to the murderer Ludwig Schmidt.

"Perhaps in retrospect," my mother says, "it was better you didn't see him as he lay dying. The tumor spread to his brainstem, and he lay staring blankly, his mouth open, tears pouring from his eyes."

I said nothing. "You surely remember the day that you went into the basement. Here, this is for you," my mother said, handing me a small box. "Here, take all the photos and documents. I think, if you'll allow me to say this, there is value in learning the history. Your connection with Sarah Eisenberg was special from a very early age not merely because of her remarkable personality and your love of her as a teacher, but because of how much you love the subject she taught."

Every sentence she speaks sounds hesitant, apologetic. This is Marta, I remind myself, who almost lost her daughter.

"I noticed," she continues, "that when folks grow older, they become like dogs, or birds. I feel as though I've become a bird resting on a weak branch right before it breaks off."

To me it seems that her body has indeed shriveled. We stood embracing for a minute. I went into the house to finish packing my suitcase. The flight would depart early the next morning. The day after I land, Talya and Eddie's wedding would take place.

That evening, before flying back to Israel, I went through some of the documents and photos. They smelled of leather, as they did that day I went into the basement and saw the black whip.

But this time I didn't faint. Our souls and psyches toughen up.

In Lublin Ghetto Deputy Commander Ludwig Schmidt's diary I found recurring entries relating to chess.

"This morning I'll be playing the Eastern Poland Youth Champion, a zhid, Yossi-Yosseleh Zilberman."

"Yosseleh taught me a move called The Shoemaker's Mate. This little zhid is definitely very gifted."

"To help Yosseleh survive Operation Erntefest, I moved him to the Fortress. He's worth it."

Diary entries for April 1944 note Schmidt's forthcoming vacation.

"I told Yossi that I'm going home to Heidelberg for Easter. He asked that if he's not here when I return, the name on his gravestone (he thinks he's going to have a burial plot!) should say 'Yossi Zilberman-Karlinski' to honor his grandfather Rabbi Karlinski."

Boarding the plane for Israel after a sleepless night, I try to stay focused on Talya Karlinski's marriage to Eddie. Of course I won't share this information with Talya on her wedding day! Who knows when I will, because that means also telling her that my father was directly involved in murdering her family, her grandparents, her aunts and uncles, her cousins, her nieces and nephews, and dozens more members of the wonderful Zilberman-Karlinski families, Lublin residents for centuries.

"What's up, Sophie?" Talya asks.

"Why're you asking?"

"You're staring at me as though it's the first time you've ever seen me," Talya laughs.

"I guess I'm just tired from the flight. Let's get your hair and makeup done like a sweet, pretty bride deserves."

I fight back my tears, but it's true, it's as though I'm seeing her, really seeing her, for the first time in my life. Suddenly I catch the similarity between her and the boy from the photo album, the boy in the torn sweater sitting at the chess board across from Ludwig, his chin in his palm as he gazes intently at the game. Talya has the exact same way of resting her head on her palm. The exact same furrow of concentration on her brow. The same huge brown eyes ringed in thick black eyelashes as though permanently mascaraed.

"You're getting over-excited," Talya chuckles at me. "I'm so certain that Eddie is the right man for me, the one who completes my soul. And I also feel much calmer for having shown him the way this dress flares," she says, spinning around the room in small waltz steps, holding the air as though holding out the hem of an invisible dress.

"No time for pantomime dances now. Get in the shower already and wash your hair. I brought my mother's blow dryer!" I pretend to give her stern orders.

"Deutschland, Deutschland, Über Alles," she sings at me in a cheeky squeaky voice as she heads for the bathroom.

Right after I met Noah at the Jewish Agency offices in Kurfürstendamm Strasse in Berlin, and explained a bit too effusively, my voice trembling, why I wanted to join a kibbutz in Israel, his retort came with a slightly cynical smile. "But you've got everything here. Isn't Deutschland uber alles?"

Quietly, my head bowed, I answered. "When I was sixteen I discovered my father was a murderer. I can't live here any longer, and definitely can't raise my future family here."

A weighty silence ensued. I looked up and saw his eyes were moist. Later he told me that it was the first time anyone had spoken directly about the past, and he could barely hold his tears back.

Noah waited for a month after our meeting in the office. On the day after I completed high school he phoned and invited me to take a walk with him. The stroll ended with us sitting on the banks of the Spree River.

"Can you believe it? The stars seem so far away, millions of light years, but in the future it might be discovered that they're actually much closer," he said in his rich bass which, already in our first meeting, penetrated my heart.

"I've already discovered that everything's so much closer. I'm a girl from Heidelberg, taking a walk with a Jewish guy born in a kibbutz in Israel. Technically we're even further than light years from each other."

"You're the most mature young woman of your age I've ever come across, not just from Heidelberg but in the world. How do you think I speak German like it's my mother tongue? My parents are Berlin born but escaped in time and came to Israel."

Noah turned to face me, placing his hand over mine. "I've never felt such a strong wish as I feel with you not only to listen to another but also talk about my past. If you like, I'll arrange a place for you where I live, in Kibbutz Ein Yam."

The scent from Talya's shampoo filled the room. She always loved a faint background of eucalyptus but after falling in love with Eddie she was a bit amazed at the mystical connection between her and the scent of eucalyptus originating from Australia, Eddie's country of birth.

"Ready!" she laughed, sitting on a chair in front of the mirror.

"Good. Now let's get you all prettied up!" I said.

"Take it easy." She flashed me a smile, the big open one that Noah calls the ultimate Tzabar smile, using the nickname for Israelis. It's the same smile that roused something in my heart when I met her standing next to the big dishwasher in the industrial kitchen adjacent to the dining hall, the day after I arrived in the kibbutz.

EDWARD PERKINS:
6 September 1970

She tries the dress on. It seems that kibbutz weddings don't prohibit the groom from seeing the bride's dress in advance. Her mother helped her with the purchase because the kibbutz budget wasn't enough for the one she wanted, which she spotted in the window of "Israel Fashion" in Weizmann Street, Givatayim.

"Don't you love this dress, Eddie?" she asks, opening her big eyes even wider in h er excitement.

"Yes, my doe-eyed dear," I say, hugging her, knowing she's the love of my life.

Talya was born thousands of kilometers from Melbourne. Talya, with her doe eyes, and her little nose that crinkles when she's displeased. I have no doubt at all. Talya feels like home to me. I'm as sure of that as I was sure at thirteen, with a kind of absolute certainty, that even though Johnny and his friends didn't stop making fun of my decision to visit my kindergarten teacher in hospital that day instead of going out with them to have fun, I'd keep my promise to Rosa and celebrate the day she called Bar Mitzvah with her.

"Eddie, Eddie, where are you?" I hear Talya's voice, "lost in chess moves again?"

"I'm right here, sweetheart."

"I want to spin," Talya says as she does, in big twirls to show me the white dress with the hand painted ornamentation in green and blue on the bodice and sleeves.

"Look at how this cloche opens!" she claps her hands.

"What's a cloche?" I ask, starting to turn with her, singing "hold me cloche…"

"I don't know where it comes from. Maybe it's Polish? I'll have to ask my mother."

"Once, years ago when I was little, I had a friend who Mum said came from Poland and I remember we danced and said words in Polish that I didn't understand."

Talya's big eyes are asking a lot of questions.

"There's no time now but I promise to tell you about Viki and her grandfather. He came from a small city next to the Gdansk and told me that hefty laborers build ships there."

"Ha!" Talya says. "Abba spoke about Gdansk and a shipyard laborer, Lech Walesa, who organized the laborers' strike there. Abba said that Walesa would become Poland's leader once it frees itself from the clamp of communism."

She hugs me tight. "Unbelievable. Just unbelievable."

"What is?" I can barely breathe, she's squeezing me so tightly.

"That you've come from the other side of the world to talk to me about things my father mentioned shortly before he passed away. How does a guy from Melbourne even know that Gdansk exists?"

She laughs even though tears roll down her cheeks. I sit her down on the sofa and stroke her hair

"Yes, more of that," she says.

That's my Talya, who says "Don't stop!" when we're making love.

My Talya who said, the very first time I kissed her lips so long that it seemed I'd stopped breathing, "I don't always like to say, 'making love.' Sometimes I like to say 'fucking,' which is like feeling the fluttering with the word's letters. Words need to be precise, you know."

After easing herself off me and curling up against my body she always had some kind of question.

"Remember how Oliver Twist asked for another bowl of gruel in the orphanage?" It took me time to get used to the way she referred to historic and literary figures as though they were in her circle of friends.

"Can you imagine it? Janusz Korczak going with the Jewish orphans from Warsaw Ghetto on the train?" I must've given her a blank look. "Don't you know anything about Janusz Korczak?"

Naked, she went to sit at the desk and wrote a list which she titled "Twenty Must-Read Books," laughed, and came back to curl up next to me.

"You met Rosa the kindergarten teacher for sure. Maybe in some other life but you met her," I said, feeling my stomach cramp. "Didn't I ever tell you about her? She always said I've got a Jewish soul. I never really understood what she meant by that. I just knew that I loved the stewed fruit, cooled and served as desert, which she made and called 'compote' so much that I insisted Mum learn how to make it too."

Johnny laughed his head off that day but Mum hugged me. "You're the sweetest boy in the world and you have excellent taste when it comes to food."

"You've got excellent taste in food? But you're always asking to have that horrible Vegemite spread sent from Australia. Although it's true that you love my mother's noodle soup, which gives her such a thrill. Whoever would've believed that Edward Perkins from Melbourne loves Polish Jewish cooking!"

Talya laughed as she headed for the shower. When she comes out, I watch as she sits, naked, combing her long hair. I take the purple brush from her hand and slowly comb through it, the scent of eucalyptus wafting across the room.

Rosa would take us to the grove near the kindergarten and explain that there are seventy-four types of eucalyptus trees on our massive, unique island continent. I tell Talya this.

"Yes, my love. This new shampoo I bought has eucalyptus extract in it of a kind meant to strengthen hair. I love you combing my hair but you've got to get ready. Noah and Sophie are waiting for us to join them for dinner," she reminds me.

By then I knew without a trace of doubt that I wanted to live with her.

Now she's laughing at me again. "We'll be late for our own wedding! Hurry up! Go and dress. The guests will be here soon. We need to get to the poolside area. Karl is waiting for you at Sophie and Noah's."

TALYA KARLINSKI:
August 1973

Everything's packed. Yishai is playing with the yellow giraffe that Noah and Sophie bought for his first birthday. Ein Yam was my home from the day I arrived with the agricultural settlement group. Ein Yam is where Abba, Herman, is buried. It's where I met the love of my life. Ein Yam is where I walked through wheatfields and watched the most beautiful sunsets in the world changing from deep orange to fuchsia-purple. They're never yellow-gold. And Ein Yam is where I learned to think that no war, no matter how just and important it seems, is worth it compared to the unpretentious babbling of a baby.

In this kibbutz I gave birth to our son, Yishai.

"Does that name mean the same as Shai?" Eddie asked.

"The word 'shai' is in both names. It means gift. The difference is that one of the names has an additional 'yi' in front which indicates two words blended together: 'yesh shai,' the gift has come. Not only your name is linked to royalty, Edward. Yishai, which you know in English as Jesse, is the Biblical King David's father."

"Here's another parallel. Our Yishai is the son of the 'Moabite' Perkins dynasty. Yishai Karlinski Perkins, son of Edward, to whom Talya said: 'Your people are my people and wherever you go, so too shall I.' So here I am, following you to Australia."

Eddie laughed and came over to me, hugging me tight, kissing my lips firmly.

"Don't worry, my pretty doe, Australia will fall in love with you and you with it."

Every day I fall in love with him again.

Kibbutz Ein Yam's secretariat decided not to approve the budget for Eddie's studies after he was accepted into the Faculty of Medicine at Tel Aviv University. The secretariat was represented by a young woman with a mole on her chin and ruddy skin on her neck. In our youth movement meetings she'd snort when she disliked something the group leader said, and he'd turn to me, saying, "We haven't heard your view yet, Talya."

Sophie reported that in the kibbutz members meeting, that young woman presented a point of opposition. "Talya's studies were paid for by the kibbutz. Let Eddie wait a bit. And anyhow, why do those two think they should be given everything?"

"Was it made clear that Eddie would be studying at his own expense? His parents said they'd be willing to pay the costs," I said to Sophie.

"I explained that," Sophie answered, "and then a discussion began about the loss of workdays." Sophie's face was red with anger as she twisted the end of her scarf around her finger.

"Sophie," I said, and gently slipped the cloth away from her finger which was slowly turning blue. "My dear friend, don't worry. I won't let Eddie forego his lifelong dream. He completed a year of studies at Sydney University but under the serendipitous influence of your cousin Karl, who to this day I thank, decided to come with him to Israel. We'll probably decide to swap the Holy Land for the Land of Oz."

I laughed, because the renowned nickname for Australia fit so perfectly into the joke. I hugged Sophie hard. I could feel that lump in my throat which used to appear every time Abba-Herman told me stories about Yosseleh and I held the tears back so he wouldn't stop the story, and only after he finished I'd begin to cough and run to quickly hold my head above the toilet bowl. I don't remember how old I was when the cough turned into one accompanied by phlegm, and which would bother me for the rest of my life.

"What does that madame with the mole have against you?" Sophie asked as she wiped away the tears collecting in the corners of her eyes.

"I guess it's a kind of envy from way back when we were in the youth movement together. Don't even bother giving her another thought."

"A pity," Sophie summed up in her practical, very forthright manner.

Whenever she does that I have to silence a little voice in my head that says, "Don't forget she's German."

Eddie was accepted for medical studies at Sydney University. Some of his earlier courses were recognized as credits even though seven years had passed. Groups of friends had begun visiting, all asking us to reconsider, promising they'd raise the issue again at the kibbutz meetings, or suggesting that perhaps we could go as kibbutz movement delegates for a while. I could represent the kibbutz movement while Eddie studied. I was really touched by the amount of love people were showing to us but understood very clearly that our place for the next few years would not be on kibbutz. The die had been cast.

Karl, who'd stayed to work in Australia after earning his degree, really wanted us to live near him. "You'll love it here in Darlinghurst, Talya. It's full of bookstores, restaurants, and has a great cosmopolitan atmosphere. It's where I first met Eddie when we both studied at uni," he said in a phone call with us. I already knew that "uni" was Ozzie slang for university. Eddie had explained that Australians like to shorten everything! "I'm sure leaving Ein Yam is really tough," he added, and I could feel that choking in my throat again.

Beth, Eddie's Mum, recommended a different neighborhood, closer to the beach and more suited, in her view, to a family with a child.

Friends keep coming to make their farewells.

"There'll always be a place for you here," Noah says, "but how're you feeling, Talya?"

"Inside, I know that the kibbutz is basically a group of people who wanted to do a lot of good, to restrain evil. And on the way some became a little more bourgeois, forgetting how we all walked in the open fields and enjoyed the beauty and miracles of nature."

"Like in Leah Goldberg's poem, the one you love so much." He quotes the verse to me: "And you inhaled the soothing scent of the furrow."

"Yes," I agreed. "But some have forgotten the simplicity we sought and are focusing on who does or doesn't deserve what. Don't worry though, Noah. I'll always leave a bit of myself in this place, like in a dream I'd never imagined. It's where I met the love of my life, and where Yishai wakes in the morning and hears birds chirping, and the imprint of his little feet mark the paths."

With the warmth that expresses everything we've experienced he embraces me for a few moments, moves away, turns and leaves.

"He's learned to be like Sophie. Practical, to the point, no wavering," I mutter to Yishai, who's still talking to his yellow giraffe.

EDWARD PERKINS:
August 1973

Everything's packed. My winter clothes, which Talya organized, are in the blue suitcase. She rolls shirts and sweaters up like sausages to save space. In the outer compartment she stored my scarf, gloves and knitted beanie.

"Yes, I remembered August is winter in the Land of Oz and you'll catch a cold if you don't keep yourself warmly wrapped," she explained.

And I remembered her turning up suddenly at the inter-kibbutz chess competition held in Ein Yam last January, and the kerosene heaters didn't really manage to heat the members' club.

"I don't want Beth Perkins getting more upset with me than she usually is over you taking such a huge hiatus in your med studies and staying in Israel. She's always worrying about your throat," Talya adds. "I remember exactly what she told me during her last visit: 'I'm not sure that nowadays Russel would've decided to remove Eddie's tonsils but when he was little, that was the accepted way to deal with recurring throat infections.' That's exactly what she said!"

Talya laughs as she repeats Mum's words and dances around me, winding the scarf around my neck. And kissing my cheek. The tall chess player from Kibbutz HaOgen had gazed at Talya with a blend of disbelief and amazement.

"What, haven't you ever seen a woman who worries about her guy?" Talya gave him her winning smile. "Why don't we introduce you to one of our group's girls?" she suggested to him as she turned to leave the club.

"Well, we could certainly recruit you for self-confidence reinforcement workshops for our kibbutz girls, if we had such an activity," the tall guy laughed.

Suddenly I realized that in addition to her beauty and brains, one of Talya's sexiest traits was the way she was so comfortably confident, a kind of statement attesting to 'this is how I am and this is what I do.' in a small, tight-knit and judgmental society like the kibbutz it was definitely a somewhat daring and irregular mode of conduct. 'What would people say' was never something Talya feared.

For years I never lost a chess game. In every competition I entered from the age of thirteen on, I won first place. That includes competitions at uni, but that rainy afternoon in the Ein Yam clubhouse, the tall guy from HaOgen simply got me with a classic Shoemaker's Mate. My mind was so taken with my love that I forgot to protect my queen.

After we made love, or as Talya would sometimes say, our very first fuck, when we lay on our sides, her back curved against my chest, she spoke about her family.

"My cousin Yosseleh, who was the son of Hava, my father's sister, was the Polish youth chess champ. He won the tournament in 1936."

"Wow. So when can I play against him?"

There was a drawn out silence. She rose, gathered her hair in a ponytail, and started sweeping our room.

"Yosseleh was murdered in the Lublin Ghetto. Abba's entire family was murdered in the Shoah."

This was the first time she mentioned the family so directly. Later I'd come to realize that she'd speak about them in the present as though they were still alive. But her Abba, Herman, would tell her stories every night about the family members who were incinerated. Mostly, though, she focuses on Yosseleh, the genius child.

"Talya, I've got chess sets at my parents' place in Melbourne. You really don't need to pack this heavy one," I said when I picked up the especially weighty gray suitcase.

"I do, though. It's the one Abba asked his friends from Krakow to send specially for me so he could teach me. It was specifically made to replicate the one used by Rabbi Simha Bunim of Przysucha."

On one of our first dates, after I said, "That's so clever, what you just said," to one of her remarks, she burst into her contagious laughter.

"Well, remember that I'm the descendant of one of the cleverest and most original Rabbis in all Polish Hassidism!"

That began a period in which I read every book and article I could find on Rabbi Simha.

"Abba and I never finished a game because he'd start talking about Yosseleh, and his tears would begin to fall. Before he passed away, he told me that when Rabbi Simha's wife cried at her husband's bedside as he lay dying, he asked her: 'Why are you crying? After all, my whole life was nothing but the study of how to die.' After Abba passed away, not long before you and I met each other, I felt urged to preserve those memories of Yosseleh." She paused, then in a soft voice continued. "So this chess set goes with me everywhere."

"Take it. Of course you must." I held my love tight. "Lily, Rosa's daughter, is moving soon to Double Bay in Sydney. It's because of Rosa that I came with Karl to kibbutz, and to you. I'm sure you'll find mutual interests."

I didn't let Talya go yet, but instead, whispered into her ear. "I know how hard it is for you to suddenly become like a migrating bird, leaving this land which you love, but not belonging there."

Talya looked up into my eyes. Hers shone with tears of gratitude.

"Rosa made me a kind of Bar Mitzvah before she passed away. It was the day that the Eichmann Trials started. Every morning since then, I thank her for the way she eventually brought you to me."

I glance around our tiny house. Three suitcases stand ready, pushed up against the wall of what amounts to our living room. This is where Talya moved to when we married, leaving behind the tiny room in the neighborhood that the kibbutz called "Atid," the future, a collection of small scale housing where other singles who were in the original Ein Yam group still lived. This tiny house is where our love matured, where our son Yishai was born. It is decorated in her own eclectic style, with warm colors, an antique makeup table she inherited from her mother's uncle, and a modernistic glass table. Crimson curtains. A massive bookcase. Pictures everywhere.

Now the walls were bare, the shelves empty, all our

possessions packed in our suitcases. I sit on the lone chair in the living room. After almost six years away I'm about to return to the familiar whiffs of sea, to Coogee's rocks, to Bondi Beach, which is like none other I the world, to Darlinghurst's book-nooks. To the square yard in Sydney University, built in 1850, and the stunning neo-Gothic structures studding the campus considered one of the most beautiful in the world.

"I needed to complete my medical studies in London but you're a lucky fellow, you can do yours in Sydney," Dad said to me after I shared our plans to return. When I told Talya that I'd been accepted for medical studies and that some of my earlier subjects would be recognized, she smiled.

"We're a team," she said. "You supported my studies. My turn to be there for you now."

"But you were planning on starting your Master's. Maybe we should postpone my studies until you've done that?"

"Med studies need many years. I'll get back to mine when the time comes. Yishai needs at least one parent around full time."

That's what my doe-eyed love said, and I know it'll be hard for her not to be the usual Talya in the center of things, admired, smart, a prominent force in her social circles.

I console myself with the thought that knowing Talya, she'll achieve her goals despite being in a new country.

"I'm going out to say bye to a few friends," she says, leaning over me with Yishai in her arms so I can kiss her, and him.

TALYA KARLINSKI:
September 1973

The sea here is different. But the sea is the same sea. The sea embraces our new home in Sydney. Karl found us this place in the suburb of Coogee, a charming place and not far from Bondi Beach. I watch the huge waves smashing against the rocks and think of Tchernikovsky's poem, the one we studied in Grade 9. Even though Spring's arrived I'm still cold, wrapped in Eddie's soft gray sweater and warm socks, listening to Yishai mutter and gurgle as he builds a city from blocks and sets the giraffe in its center.

"Giraffi, do you want more friends?" he asks in the sweetest tone.

Tears well in my eyes. Exactly three years ago Eddie and I married on kibbutz. I never felt alone there. But Eddie's immersed in his studies as though he's just dived into deep water.

Eddie's cousin Rachel will be here soon. When she met me on Sunday she came right up close to me and leaned in towards me with a question. "D'you think we're doing enough about the environment, and saving the planet?"

I thought about Uri and Avner, two beloved friends of mine, brothers who were killed, one in the Golan

Heights, the other in Sinai, during the Six-Day War. I thought about Shmulik, my brilliant high school friend who succumbed to shell shock after the battle over Ammunition Hill in Jerusalem where he saw his mates and fellow soldiers butchered by soldiers from the Jordanian Legion. When I visited him in Tel Hashomer Hospital's orthopedic department where he lay recovering from an operation which amputated his badly injured right leg from the knee down, he spoke of how lucky he was that it was only from the knee down. "Talinka," he sobbed, "I still don't understand how everyone else was killed but this morning I ate yogurt, a boiled egg and fresh cucumber for breakfast."

"And no olives?" I smiled, hoping for a brief laugh or even a smile on his face.

I thought about my mother, who stood in the doorway, the brown leather bag dangling from her wrist, the one Herman had sewn for her back when they could still look at each other, and Clara, the neighbor, stood in front of her. At virtually the same moment they'd both said the same thing.

"No air raid siren is going to upset us! We're not going down into any shelters. Been there done that, as they say, when the Nazis were after us. The most important thing is that the *tashik*," a bag, in Yiddish, "holds enough money and jewelry."

But sweet Rachel lives a very different life, and her war is saving the planet. Is that, perhaps, the right way to look at the world? The normal way?

"Of course," I answer, "and Australia's leading the way to improve the environment and make sure to bring it to all western governments' attention. Even in Israel, which is very busy with issues of existential security, they're starting to insert classes on environmental protection into school curriculums."

"No kidding!"

And from that conversation on, she was in touch with me almost daily.

"Talya, get dressed quick. Beth will be here soon to look after Yishai. And you're coming with me to free Sam the whale who got stuck near Bondi Beach. We've got to do everything we can to push him back into the water, and we've also got to constantly keep him moist. I heard that he's pretty exhausted."

The doorbell rings. Beth's there, tall, sapphire blue eyes, blond ponytail twisted and caught up with a big clip. Pearl earrings, a pearl necklace, beige pants, cream shirt, a London Fog brand beige coat. Pale pink lipstick. Long fingers. A wedding ring on her right hand, a medium sized diamond ring next to it.

Her smile is warm, enveloping. She gives Rachel and me a quick hug each and immediately sits down on a cushion next to Yishai.

"Who lives in the house you built?" she asks him softly.

"Giraffi!" Yishai squeals and the two of them burst into laughter.

It's comforting to know that Yishai's in good hands, the best in the world. The perfect mother has turned into the perfect Granny. But when will I feel comfortable here in Australia? Will I ever feel comfortable here? A morning passes, another and another, a tower of blocks, Lego buildings, a walk on the wonderful Coogee beachfront with its natural pools holding seawater and people coming to swim in them every morning, always making a point of leaving the area clean. Rachel also comes here frequently, joining protesters wanting the government to clean up the rivers. She collects plastic trash from the beaches and joins marches demanding recyclable materials.

I, who just yesterday, so it seems, sat in the berry tree thinking I was Tarzan's Jane, am beginning to crumble like the western wall of this house, peeling from so much seeping moisture that even the pictures covering the wall are showing signs of mold. I need to clean them. But what for?

Who'll look after little Yishai? I can depend on Eddie but what would happen to his dream of studying medicine? I'm sitting facing the physician in the Coogee clinic as he explains that I'm not having a heart attack.

"The EKG is fine, Mrs. Karlinski Perkins," he says. "Are you Dr. Russell Perkins' daughter-in-law? He told me that Edward's back in Australia with his wife and baby son. We're longtime friends from med school." He pauses and nods reassuringly. "What you experienced is an anxiety attack. It's no easy thing to move to a new country. I suggest you find some kind of activity or employment. It will go a long way to helping you."

Eddie returns at night and tells me about the amygdala deep in the brain's temporal lobes, the central area linked to emotion and which produces emotional memory, as he holds me in his embrace.

"You've got the most developed amygdala in the world!" he chuckles. "You just smell a carrot and instantly remember the meals you ate in kindergarten! Anyhow, the class on brain anatomy is amazing." He releases me. "What? What is it, my gorgeous Talya?"

And then the tears in the corners of my eyes turn into uncontrollable sobbing. "Maybe I made a mistake. Maybe this isn't for me? I so long to be the Talya who's known, who belongs, and it's killing me."

Eddie holds me tight, gently wiping the tears away, and kisses me long and lovingly, stroking my back, my breasts, lifting me in his arms, gently placing me on the bed.

"You are the only reason I can breathe, my love." He gazes into my eyes. "If you're not feeling comfortable here, let's go back. I'm with you. remember? Wherever you go..." he quotes to me again as he weaves his long pianist's fingers into mine. I breathe deeply, the way I learned in kundalini yoga, and rest my head on his chest.

"When you came to Ein Yam you said that before you met me, you felt odd, strange, out of place, and you said please way too often, and you apologized all the time, and people's eyes opened wide because they were wondering, who is that guy?!"

"Yes, and then you appeared, and said that people love it when someone comes from a different world. People are curious, and that's what will happen with you too. We're still at the start of things. I'm sorry that I got so immersed in my own stuff. Tomorrow I'll look around for options that might be good for you. I've no doubt that very soon you'll feel like your usual Talya Karlinski in Oz too," he grinned.

How is it that my guy manages to inject the Perkins

family tranquility into my veins? I asked myself, and fell asleep.

In the morning I dress Yishai and tell him we're going for a walk around the neighborhood, looking for the kindergartens recommended by Granny Beth and Auntie Rachel.

"Let's take Giraffi!" he chortles as he hugs it tight.

The phone rings. "This is the secretary of Dr. Ruth Weiss, Principal of Moriah Jewish Day School in Sydney. We'd be pleased if you'd come in tomorrow at 10 am for a job interview."

"Talya, do you remember how many times you helped me with everything that needed taking care of in Ein Yam?" Eddie asked when I try to prevent him from missing class so that he can accompany me to the interview. "So, please, let me do this. It doesn't detract from your independence. It could simply get the ball rolling more smoothly."

He drives me to the school. I kiss him and whisper in his ear. "I'm fine."

"SO Israeli!" he says loudly.

"Full disclosure," the school principal says, shaking my hand and gesturing to a chair. Dr. Weiss is a short woman with green, cat-like eyes. "Lily, my childhood friend from Melbourne, told me about Eddie's unique connection with her mother Rosa, his kindergarten teacher, and asked me to meet with you. Tell me a little about your field."

"I studied history and theater, completing my degree

with Honors, but I haven't really taught before, although when I began my master's I taught tutorials at university on Ramkovsky, known as King of the Lodz Ghetto. I was Professor Yehuda Bauer's assistant. He's an expert on the Shoah. My plans were to develop an academic career."

She gave me a penetrating gaze.

"So you postponed your studies to allow your husband to study. No simple decision," she said, nodding.

I can feel the lump taking shape in my throat. I'm hoping I won't burst into tears.

6-17 October 1973

"You're laughing the way you used to when you and Eddie visited his parents in Melbourne. I remember being amazed at how free and wonderful your laugh was," Lily says to me.

"I admit it. I've started to feel a bit more at home here and you've got a lot to do with that," I said, hugging her. "I'm so happy you came to spend Yom Kippur with me."

Eddie went to his study group. Beth will take Yishai from kindergarten. There's an easy routine to things, like there used to be. My body's feeling lighter. We walk along the Coogee beachfront, the wind blowing through Lily's gorgeous hair.

"Your hair's like sheaves of wheat," I say and Lily laughs briefly.

"My mother always said I'd have survived because of my Aryan looks," she says softly. "From the earliest I can remember, that statement has been lodged under the surface of my skin. An incomprehensible statement, without any explanation. It took years for me to understand it. To this day it rouses a kind of anger, an aggravation which I also felt in my childhood. Who says things like that to a little girl living in Australia among eucalyptus trees and ballet classes?"

"But her compote was wonderful, according to Eddie," I try to lighten the tone.

"True, and she was a wonderful Mum, and Eddie was privileged to have enjoyed her love. The anger that surfaces is more like a reflex, not a true, live emotion, because what can one expect from a woman whose grandparents, sisters, cousins, teachers, neighbors that she played with, the shoemaker around the corner who repaired her school shoes, and her piano teacher, all rose to heaven through the smoking chimney stacks of the Majdanek concentration camp."

And I froze.

"I didn't know Rosa's family was from Lublin."

"Eddie must've forgotten to tell you," Lily says. "But what difference does it make? They all died."

"My father's family was from Lublin. Every night before I fell asleep he'd tell me stories about how pretty the city was, about the river, about his older sister Hava, and mostly about Yosseleh, her brilliant son. And what happened to them all…"

"Sydney has a very active community of Jews formerly from Lublin. I'll take you to one of their events someday. But now, a moment of relaxation," Lily says, signaling to come with her where the waves splash onto the sand.

Both of us draw in deep breaths, raising our hand up, breathing out slowly, bringing our palms together and lowering our arms, as longtime yoga practitioners do.

"When I was in the Habonim summer camp," Lily says, referring to one of the worldwide Jewish youth movements, "we learned the song 'Eli, Eli' by Hannah Senesh."

I nod. I know that Senesh, who lived in Kibbutz

Sdot Yam, joined the British forces, trained as a Special Operations recruit, and parachuted in behind Nazi enemy lines during WWII as part of a covert operation to rescue Hungarian Jewry from the Nazis' Final Solution. Lily begins to sing. I join her in what over time has become a kind of prayer. We stand there before waves rolling in from the Pacific Ocean. An hour from now we would learn that the place which inspired Senesh's poetic words would soon be pounded with air raid sirens signaling war. But for now we return home and sit watching the sun sink into darkness as we sip gin and tonic. My first Yom Kippur in Australia is over. In the nearby Greek restaurant typically Greek music is playing: an atmosphere of vibrancy pervades.

Lily turns the TV on. The time difference between Australia and Israel means we're now watching the evening news. "The Egyptian army has just crossed the Suez Canal," the broadcaster announces.

Right then Eddie calls. "It's war," he says breathlessly, "I'm coming home right now."

And I'm far away in my thoughts, there, at home, remembering the gloom in Noah's eyes when he returned from the Six Day War, and Shmulik's shell shock.

"Five or six days at most," Lily says.

But I know that this time it's a very different situation. "It'll take much longer than that," I whisper .

She hugs me in the doorway before she turns to leave. "But thank goodness you and Eddie and Yishai are here."

Her words cut through my soul. My brethren are fighting, and I've just watched a cerise Coogee sunset. A breeze makes the bells Eddie hung above the window tinkle. It seems to me that the restaurant turned the music up louder. They're probably dancing inside.

Far from the sirens, far from the jets slamming through the air, far from the radios updating nonstop. Far from the names of the fallen. Far from the fears that paralyze us. Just a month ago I was seriously wondering if we shouldn't be going back home, but today Mrs. Karlinski is a Jewish History and Hebrew Language teacher for 9th graders at Sydney's Jewish day school, Moriah College.

"Mrs. Karlinski, the class on the false prophet Shabbtai Tzvi was fascinating!"

"The poem 'Eli, Eli' moved me deeply and you sing so nicely."

"My Mum lived for a few years in Israel and really wants to meet you even before parents' day. Is that possible?"

I'm being enveloped in warmth and love. The feeling of otherness is slowly dissipating. Yishai goes to the Montessori kindergarten in Bronte, a suburb not too far from us. He builds towers from prisms, plays the drums, eats raisins from small packages, sings Mozart's songs of spring. Leaves me easily at the gate with a quick "Bye, mummy" and runs into the arms of Claire, the kindergarten teacher with the velvet voice. But there, back home, there's a war, and loss, and blood.

Tomorrow after the students talk about how they handled the twenty-four hours of no food and no drink on Yom Kippur, the holy fast day, ending with the Shofar being sounded, we will discuss the war that has just begun in faraway Israel.

The first call after war broke out came from Sophie.

Just like after Abba passed away, her voice was energetic, her words to the point and practical when she helped me shake myself out of my mourning and begin socializing again. And, unbeknown to us all, meet the love of my life. Now, too, her words are practical.

"Talya, my dearest friend, don't even think of coming back here right now."

She noted that I'd just started to get used to living in Australia, that I was sounding more comfortable and happier recently.

"This will be a tough war, longer, but we'll win," Noah says on the phone. "See you, our lovely Talya. I'm heading south to join my unit. Your practical friend has packed everything I need and then some!" he laughs.

"Noah. Look after yourself," I say.

"Sure."

From the start of this war news comes in waves. It sounds like the Destruction of the Third Temple. I go to school quickly. I hurry back home and stay glued to the radio and TV. Once a day I catch up with Sophie.

The phone rings. Rona, my friend from our earliest days in the youth movement and on Kibbutz Ein Yam, our ideology driven days. Secretary of Kibbutz Ein Yam. I can feel my heartbeat pulsing everywhere in my body. I sit down even before she says anything.

"Talya, you need to sit down…" I know what she'll say. There's something about her intonation, the quickness of her words. Noah was killed in Sinai. Actually, right after crossing the Suez. Actually, in the area called Sinai Farm. Actually, you probably heard: it was two days ago." No, I hadn't heard. "The paratroopers set up a floating pontoon bridge allowing the tanks to cross. Noah was the company commander, you know. The soldiers were under attack by a ton of live ammunition right from the start."

I feel as though Rona hasn't taken a breath in all that time.

"Rona, Rona, stop for a second. I don't need all the details!" I sob deeply in a voice even I don't recognize. She goes silent.

"Sophie? How's Sophie?" I whisper into the phone.

"When she opened the door to the military officers and me, before she gave us a chance to speak, she took one look at us and said she needed to wash the house, and began pouring buckets of water on the floor and dragging it out through the door with the big squeegee. We had to move away. I sent Hannah the nurse over to her to give her a sedative. She's surrounded by friends. We don't leave her on her own for a second."

"She's going to give birth in two months!" I said, feeling helpless.

"Yes. She'll call you when she's ready. Look after yourselves."

Rona ended the call. But I sat there for a very long time just holding the phone in my hand, as though not knowing what to do with it until the buzz coming from the ended call burrowed into my brain and I put the receiver back down.

"Sometimes," I say aloud to myself, "it happens in life that there's no explanation for what takes place. No answer to the question." How is it, I ponder, that of all people, Sophie, a German, who found love, who became part of the kibbutz, of the country, in some instances seeming even more solidly anchored there than others born in Israel, lost what was dearer to her than anything else in her life to this country at war? Is It some kind of spiritual retribution for the abominable acts of her nation of birth?

"I'm not going to let Rachel talk to me about saving whales," I sob as Eddie gently eases me into an armchair and hands me a gin and tonic.

"I have to be there," I say.

"You'll go as soon as the war's over. There's a turn in the tide. Israel's starting to win on all fronts. Crossing the Suez was critical," Eddie says.

"I have to."

"Of course you will. When it's over and safer," he repeats in a firm but gentle voice.

"But I must!" I weep.

A heap of small screams builds up in my gut. They want to break out. Edvard Munch's painting surfaces in my mind. I so badly want to stay out of this cycle of fate. I want to be Beth Perkins, I want to be Yishai, even Eddie: to feel that my life is here, in this calm place, which is doing a lot of good for my family and for me.

The man I love, who is so attentive to my needs, spoke with a tone of authority I've never heard before. Indeed, he is my true anchor.

"Come, my sweet Talya," he says, and I curl up next to him, feeling his palms stroke my back, reaching that point that rouses me, and I turn, kissing him.

I don't want words.

I just want to feel him inside me.

SOPHIE SCHMIDT
16 October 1974

They explained that Israel Defense Forces fallen are buried in the military cemetery. I insisted that they bury Noah here, at home, in Ein Yam.

A year has passed.

How do I know?

Rona, the kibbutz secretary, came to me a week ago asking if I had any ideas for conducting a memorial service for Noah since he 'left.'

"Left? What on earth does that means?"

"It's a euphemism to express the loss of someone, their death," Rona answered quietly.

"A year since Noah, my love, my friend, my husband, father of our daughter Sarah who he never managed to meet, was killed!" I spat the words out. Heaving sobs came from deep inside me, as they did when I woke from my crazed sleep at Sarah Eisenberg's house in Berlin. I was the fleeing German again. I'm sure words in German escaped my lips too.

I could feel my face burning. Fury coursed through every cell in my body. I could see the shock on Rona's face. She tried to hug me. I wriggled free from the clumsy attempt at affection and sat heavily on a chair, then in one go gulped down the glass of water she handed me.

Once I got really annoyed with Noah and spilled my heart out to Talya. She told me about her mother's frenzied attacks of fury. Then they found a growth, called pheochromocytoma, on the adrenal gland connected to her kidney. The pheo, as they called it, would make her blood pressure peak and cause these attacks. But after she was operated on, Talya said, the body rebalanced and she once again became that same Mrs. Karlinski with full self-control. Oh, and control over her surroundings.

"Pheo. That's your new nickname," Talya had laughed wildly at me, mussing my hair, "except that I know it's not because of your adrenals. It's because you're German! Sophie Pheo, Noah is a wonderful guy and he loves you to bits," Talya's arms wound around me, calming me.

"Talya used to sit with me and tell me which song was suited to which musical composition. I miss her so much." The voice coming from my own mouth didn't sound familiar at all. It was much too whiney.

"I miss her too, actually," Rona said, glancing at her watch. "But she's not here. So maybe you could write a few words, if you're able, if you want to, and I'll take care of everything else for the ceremony."

"It's okay," Noah whispers in my ear, "drop all the pressure. Just look after our Sarah and plan your trip to Australia."

"Noah! How'd you get here?"

"I took the green jeep from the cotton fields in the valley near the bananas. I came to make sure the picking's finished before the rains. After all, the keys were in the ignition. Remember when we were sitting on the Spree

River's banks in Berlin and I said you'd never be alone?"

"Sophie, Sophie, hello? You listening?" Rona says to me. "Can we agree that you'll write a short something for the memorial and I'll be responsible for arranging everything else?"

The same calming bass, like back when I knew I'd be going with him to Israel. I caress his face, my fingers digging into his ginger beard.

"Sophie?" Rona is standing in front of me. Too close to me.
"Ah, yes, yes," I say, shaking my head as though waking. "I need to get ready for my trip to Australia. Noah's recommending it'd be good, a change of place, of atmosphere."
"I'm sure the kibbutz secretariat will authorize the trip," Rona says as she gently closes the door.

"She wants to get out of the apartment as quickly as possible," Noah whispers.

I burst into laughter and went to pick Sarah up from her blue cradle.
"I won't send the cradle to Sydney even though I'm very attached to it and Noah, a genius with all things technical, became a carpenter just to make it for Yishai's birth. I'll leave it for your daughter, because I have a feeling our next will be a girl," Talya said when she began planning her and Eddie's trip to Australia.

"Noah also reckons it's a girl. He keeps stroking my belly and saying, 'my little doll.'"

It reminded me of "süße Puppe, eine süße Puppe," and I cringe inside despite the concrete wall in my soul, because Ludwig's voice nonetheless makes itself heard. His voice calling me süße Puppe penetrates my mind. When he called me Sophie, on the other hand, I knew he was about to answer a question I'd asked about studies at length and in detail.

"Did you know that the Polish word for doll is 'lalka?'" I remember him once saying, seemingly for no particular reason. "A cute word, is it not?" and then he fell silent, lost in his own world, and suddenly left the room. "I'm going to Heinrich!" he called out. The front door slammed shut.

But he came home in a good mood smelling of "Heidelberger," the beer they both loved, and kissed me good night.

"You smell!" I'd said.

"Ah, just a glass of beer, but if it bothers you, my süße Puppe, instantly and on your orders, I'll stop."

And I flung my arms around the neck of my wonderful Papa. "You can have a little bit but not too much."

"I promise," he'd answered, kissing me on the forehead.

Noah gazes into my tear-filled eyes. "Again Ludwig's gotten through the concrete barrier? Maybe that's not such a bad thing. Clean-out sets the soul free."

"I need a strong hug," I whisper.

I hear Sarah waking from her afternoon nap. My little Sarahleh, my love, who'll never be privileged to see her Abba.

"You'll show her photos and tell her little snippets and stories about Noah Mendelsohn, who called her 'doll' when she was still in the womb. And how he fell in love with you in a distant land and brought you to his kibbutz. And how he had exactly the same eyes as she has."

Talya cried into the phone. "I promise never to stop telling her about her special, wonderful Abba. Her Abba who was a hero of love, and who made such a special connection between me and her Imma that he turned me into Aunt Talya. Come, Sophie. Come and visit us here," she whispers as we end the call from one end of the earth to the other.

I clutch Sarah. Perhaps a little too tightly, because her blue eyes open wide as if to ask, "What's going on?" I lie her down on the floor to change her diaper. We have a little preliminary ritual of sounds and gurgles and tickles.

"That's what I want in life," he'd said, dancing around me in a way that always made me break into peals of laughter. "Five little Sophies just like you." And he danced "HaGalilah," a song that the early pioneers sang and danced hora to all night long.

"Little Sarah will be Sophie number one," I answered.

"Perfect name," Noah said, wrapping his arms around me.

That all happened a month after Marta wrote to let me know that Frau Eisenberg had passed away in Berlin, apparently from a heart attack. I have my own thoughts on that. In her last few letters I noticed that she sounded deeply depressed. It was even more obvious by the way she ended the last letter I received.

"Sophie, my dear,

You were like my daughter. Don't be sorry if we cannot meet again. Live a life full of meaning, a life you've wanted. Too many years of longing for our loved ones wear our souls down. That's what my life's been.

Sending you my love and admiration."

Sarah Eisenberg, who was so much more than a mother to me during the period when my whole life was in upheaval, and who was the link that enabled me to meet Noah, and connect to my identity as a person who can condemn the crimes of my family, is no more. She never overcame the loss of her husband. Throughout the entire war, hidden in the Benedictine monastery in Neuberg, she hoped he'd make it through alive. When the war was over, she searched and asked, only to discover he'd been murdered in Dachau.

"We'll fly to Aunt Talya and Uncle Eddie and Uncle Karl," I say to my little Sarah who's sitting happily in her stroller playing with a doll wearing a frilly-hemmed purple dress, the doll Talya sent from Australia.

SOPHIE SCHMIDT
December 1974

One suitcase holds all my clothes and all of Sarah's, who turned one today.

"We'll celebrate in Sydney," Talya promised.

I, Sophie née Schmidt, now Mendelsohn, had a well-mapped out life, clear, precise. A bourgeois home in pretty Heidelberg. Loving, pampering parents, proud of who they were, proud of me, giving me the best of everything. Sophie Schmidt indeed had been a happy, independent, opiniated personality, loved by her friends and people in her surroundings. Until the fall into that deep abyss of lies, the dark side of her father Ludwig's life, her mother Marta's knowledge of it. Both parents, like so many other 'good' people, closed their eyes to reality and became accomplices. I've no doubt that no one ever planned on breaching the barricade of lies and silence. Perhaps they thought that far into the future, if the truth was delivered a drop at a time under the claim of coercion into acting against their wishes, there'd be no life-changing explosion

How wrong they were.

At the sensitive stage of adolescence their opiniated daughter discovered the truth, her life instantly changing. I cut loose from my roots with the sharpest of blades and spun, slung, into complete shake-up. Where would I be now if not for my wonderful history teacher Frau Sarah Eisenberg who, after being dismissed from her position for speaking the truth, took her secrets to Berlin. She softened my fall, she was my anchor and home, through her I met Noah Mendelsohn with whom I built a new life at Kibbutz Ein Yam in Israel. She will never need to sorrow over his being taken and leaving me behind. Noah was killed in a war that now has an official title: the Yom Kippur War.

The pain fills every cell of my body, every breath I take. He's also there when I laugh with Sarah, who looks like a miniature female version of Noah, who mutters and hums, who giggles, who smiles and jumps about as soon as she hears music, just like her Mendelsohn Abba. Sitting there on the banks of the Spree River the first time we met, I asked him about his family name. He said he'd already received the family tree from a friend of his aunt Miriam, his mother's oldest sister, who managed to stay in hiding with friends in Berlin until caught and sent on the very last deportation in March 1945 from Platform 17, to her eradication.

Miriam's friend told Noah that she'd looked after the family tree all this time, and made him promise that he'd bring it to the family in Israel. "She brought it to my Jewish Agency office a week ago. When she started talking, tears began to fall from her eyes. 'Your Aunt Miriam was my best friend until the very last moment, when someone snitched about the most recent hideout,' she said as she showed me that my parents were distant cousins and both carried the Mendelson family name."

I remember bursting into tears as Noah spoke. He stroked my hair gently. "Wow. Your family belongs to probably the last few Mendelsohns who remained Jewish."

I smiled as we carefully eased the large scroll out of its embroidered sleeve and gently unrolled it in Noah's Spandaustrasse apartment.

"The truth is," he said, straightening for a moment and sighing, "that the family history never really interested me until I came to Berlin, and here too the various respectful remarks about my name make me feel even more Israeli and lucky that my parents got smart on time and decided, as early as 1934, a year after that Satan took control of the government, to leave all Berlin's supposed goodness, and to live in the Land of Israel, as they always referred to it."

"But I'm very grateful that they spoke to you in German," I said, kissing him long and firmly on the lips.

"My love," he says, "you not only dealt with the issue, not only spoke about the guilt. You stood up and went and built your own, different life. I'm so proud of you. You're almost like the founder of the Jewish Mendelshohn family's German branch." And I see him giving his ginger-bearded laugh.

"Our Saraleh has musical talent," I report to Noah on one of the night conversations we have as he hovers near my bed.

"Will you come with us to Australia?" I whisper.

"You bet!" he grins, the freckles changing shape as his cheeks bunch up. "Saraleh for sure will have freckles," I say, and fall asleep with Noah's smile wafting above me, slowly fading like the grin on Lewis Carrol's Cheshire cat.

On her first birthday, my daughter and I set out on our journey to Australia. I decided to fly via Germany. I wanted to go back to Heidelberg, a city that is now sans Ludwig. I knew that Sarah's Oma Marta would be thrilled. I needed to close this circle. Marta had for years now described herself as feeling like a bird about to fall from its perch. But I felt she deserved the opportunity to hug her granddaughter.

I watch Sarah laughing in her Oma Marta's arms, and the happiness flooding my mother's face. My heart nonetheless fills with joy, and a kind of serenity enters it that I haven't felt for years.

"Only when you reach a state of acceptance and you close the circle on your harsh life story will you be able to find release from the tremendous fury built up inside you. Your foundation is good. You received a lot of love."

So said the psychologist that Frau Eisenberg sent me to before I recommenced studies in the Jewish school in Berlin. At the time it was mumbo-jumbo to me and rekindled the anger I'd had under control but meeting with the psychologist was the precondition for staying with my history teacher. Now I understand what my sixteen year old, rebellious and distraught self couldn't. Now I'm super pleased that I decided to visit my old home.

Martha's eyes light up when she takes care of Sarah. It's a light that almost erases her constant weakness due to a heart complication which began shortly after I left the house. I'm also going to visit my beloved uncle, Heinrich, who never forgets to send me a fruit-rich Christmas cake in a colorful box printed with fir trees and children skating on the snow. Pictures from my childhood.

He's hardly changed. His hair's still identifiably blond, if somewhat faded, and only his sideburns, which I used to love playing with and messing up when I was a little girl, have gone white. I remember doing that: he'd sit me on his lap and I'd wriggle my fingers through the hair. He still seems to be solid and strong, has his broad smile and his bearhugs. He was always so very different from Ludwig, whose hair was dark, whose back was narrow, whose eyes were penetrating.

I'm Sophie Mendelsohn.

I used to be Sophie Schmidt.

"Sophie, look! Little Sarah's like me! She's got coppery hair. She'll also have the cutest freckles," Heinrich laughs.

"Ah, but her father was also freckled, and had blond hair. His parents are Berlin born," I say, trying to be relaxed as I speak, because now he's about to find out about Sarah's Berlin connection, and it won't be what he expects. "So I'm now Sophie Mendelsohn."

"Mendelsohn?" he says in a startled whisper. "Your daughter is of the Mendelsohn lineage?"

We're silent. Several minutes pass before Heinrich speaks again. "Hannah Arendt, the philosopher who currently teaches at Princeton, studied in Heidelberg and was a friend of mine. Her close friend, Ann Mendelsohn, would often visit. We were a group of students of medicine and philosophy. We talked endlessly about Moses Mendelsohn's views, and of course about Felix Bartholdy Mendelsohn and so many others in the family which mostly converted. Hannah and Ann left Germany on time. And lucky that they did. A terrible darkness prevailed here for years."

My uncle pauses. Then he gently takes my hand in his.

"My dear Sophie, we've never spoken about that truth. Admittedly I wasn't a party member because of my childhood polio, so I was left to work here in Heidelberg as a physician, luckily for me. But I was one of those who looked away. I saw the Jews disappearing, even being taken. I was silent. I carry that in my heart always, since then."

Uncle Heinrich stands up, limps over to me and hugs me for a very long time.

"I'm so proud of you," he says. "I never knew, and never asked, about your father's military service. I didn't dare pry. Most of us didn't. I didn't want to lose my brother," he says sorrowfully.

My memories of Heinrich are always linked to his laughter, his joviality, his strength. Now he cries, sobbing from somewhere deep inside. His sobs heave uncontrollably. Saraleh, in her stroller, opens her sea-blue eyes wide in surprise. I lead my uncle to his workroom and guide him into his armchair, gently stroking his head like I would a little child.

Two days later I make my farewells. Sarah was bundled in a down-filled coat and blanket. I hug Marta. Our eyes are moist. Heinrich drives me to the Heidelberg airport. I'll fly from there to Frankfurt, then to Hong Kong where I have a two-day stopover in a hotel, arranged by Karl, and from there to Sydney.

"Everyone's waiting for you," Karl tells me in a phone call to Heidelberg.

"Karl," I laugh, "you've said that ten times already!"

"You're doing the right thing, Sophie, coming to a place where you know people who love you and where there are no wars," Noah whispers in my ear, and caresses my cheek.

TALYA KARLINSKY:
23 December 1974

"It's two hours to Sophie's landing time. I think you should leave so you don't get caught in traffic jams," I hear Eddie suggesting.

"Sophie and Saraleh, Sophie and Saraleh," Yishai keeps singing. "I want the yellow shirt. I want to be like Giraffi."

I remember Noah showing up with the stuffed toy on Yishai's first birthday, before the party.

"Sophie sent me off to buy a gift. I don't get how, of all the teddy bears and dogs and other fluffy animals, I just got hooked by this giraffe, but if you don't think it's suitable, we can exchange it for a panda or something," he'd said, shrugging and grinning.

I laughed. Laughter with tears in my eyes, I laughed so hard.

Noah from the bananas, from the military jeep, from the repair to the electrical system that crashed, is standing in front of me with a giraffe and he's all red in the face and embarrassed.

"The giraffe is wonderful and very much like you," I'd said, and we hugged and laughed more. Me and my good friend. Since then the giraffe became the most precious toy in the world. Eddie and I constantly fear losing it, and where would we find another with one green eye and one brown eye, smiling at us, and without which Yishai can't fall asleep!

Noah, vibrant in every gesture, every step, every word spoken, every hug. Noah, my Noah. Prone in the ground.

"Talya?" Eddie calls from the kitchen. He cooks in a bit of a frenzy, as though needing to atone for the long days he spends invested in his studies.

"How will I know I haven't made a huge mistake that I'll always end up sorry for?" he whispers when he comes in late at night and gently tries to arouse my body.

"You're not making a mistake," I repeat. It's become a mantra. "Your med studies are your passion, your true interest. We're young. We've still got our whole lives ahead of us."

And then a silence settles in before being shattered by Noah's image. "There's no such thing in life as absolute certainty," I whisper back. "There's no way of going back to our days of innocence and feeling that kind of total joy and confidence we used to feel and knowing that we've done the best thing we could."

"But you know that you and Yishai are the best thing," Eddie says.

I know, and that's why I am all for supporting his choice, for making it our choice. Now I can hear him singing in the kitchen, composing a tune that lists all the parts of the brain, to be sure, to be completely certain, that he's ready for the next big exam and won't forget any hypophysis.

"You didn't mention the thalamus," I call out.

He laughs. "'Course I did! You just didn't hear it."

I hug this man of mine in his great big bright yellow apron that Yishai chose because it matches Giraffi.

"Abba, bye bye. Kiss Giraffi!" Yishai says and Eddie laughs, taking up his song again and beating an imaginary drum.

Two kids. That's what I have at home now. I have kids in Moriah College. I've gone back to being Talya Karlinski. Perhaps I actually have gone back to feeling comfortable in my skin, knowing my place, knowing my wishes. I can hardly believe a year's already gone by.

Sometimes after Yishai's fallen asleep I ask Eddie, "What did I say?"

"That you want to go back, and maybe you made a mistake, agreeing to come to Australia."

"And what did you answer?"

"That I'd go with you wherever you want to go. I asked you to give yourself, to give us, a bit more time."

It's a sort of ritual I conduct every so often. Eddie plays along with me. He repeats the details, never gets annoyed, never says things like "You know that already." He understands that it helps me deal with my new world. The next question is on the tip of my tongue.

"And what makes me happiest?"

"Teaching," Eddie says in a really serious tone but a huge grin. "You, Talya, who always said you were going for historical research, and if necessary you'd teach a course or two here and there in university, never realized how drawn you are to teaching. You never knew you were a fairy godmother who fascinates those high school kids. Take Amy, for example, who always went off to the music room instead of being in history class. Now she wouldn't miss it for all the world! And Jacob, who skipped almost all his classes and seemed to be attached at the hip to the janitor, is now making sure he never skips yours! The parents of 11th grade's kids wrote that letter of praise to the Principal and every single parent signed it."

He goes over to the bookshelf and picks up the local Jewish newspaper, turning to an article on the students and parents seminar I organized for Holocaust Day. "History teacher Talya Karlinski has changed the students' and parents' approach to Holocaust Day, shifting from a ceremony that had become over time fairly routine to…"

I snatch the paper from his hand. He just grins.

"Shall I read it again? And I remember how you were feeling after two weeks here," he says, summing up my ritual and tickling me in sensitive spots until I beg him to stop.

On the way to the airport I note the ibises from the corner of my eye. They pluck their way through Central Park under a strong, blue, typically Sydney summer sky.

After Eddie and I made our plans, and I acclimated to the initial pain of knowing I'd be leaving Sophie on kibbutz, Sophie had been her practical self. "Go, it's what you guys need to do. A year from now and Noah, our doll and I will visit."

"Yes, I know Noah decided you'll have a girl, and he's almost always right," I remember saying, and Sophie and I had smiled warmly but sadly to each other in that way that doesn't require words.

I grip the steering wheel. There's a salty taste in my mouth. No, not really salty. More like bland tending to salty. Who cares that he was right? I scream in my mind.

"Breathe deep," I hear Eddie whisper in my ear. "Build a wall, a screen to protect you from the difficult thoughts."

In his booster seat Yishai is altering a Hebrew song to fit the current occasion. "In the land I love the almond is blossoming, in the land I love we're waiting for a guest. We're waiting for little Saraleh."

Suddenly I leap away from my somber thoughts and break into a laugh.

"Sing with me, Imma," my sweetie says, so I do.

"Seven young women, seven mothers, seven brides at the gate."

Every night before bed he asks me to sing this song, which I love so much. He knows the words by heart.

"Sophie and Saraleh are also coming to the gate," Yishai says.

A bubble of joy envelopes me. The last time that Sophie and I celebrated the festival of Purim together, I staged a song that says, "Open the gate, open it wide, for a golden chain shall surely pass through it." We both stood in our fancy dress in front of the mirror, me laughing, Sophie forcing herself to smile.

"I'm so jealous that you've got such a carefree laugh," she said. "From earliest childhood I was raised to think that being amazed at yourself in front of the mirror is not respectable, almost invalid. When I look at myself my mind hears the voice of rebuke."

She turned to me, her eyes shining. "Where does it

come from, Talya? I've never linked this feeling to what's known as characteristically German traits."

"Perhaps," I began cautiously, "the strict education in Germany and the constant demand to uphold instructions and be precise creates a certain fear, or distancing, from being amazed at things which are considered trivial, unimportant, like trying on a dress or some new shade of pink nail polish. As though taking so much pleasure in them is superficial. A waste of time, perhaps."

"And the irony," Sophie added, "is that those nuts constantly idolized the external image of being Aryan."

She asks me to stand in profile. She stands behind me. "Look," she says pointing to the mirror, "how much longer MY nose is than your little slightly upturned one!" she says and bursts into laughter. We both do.

"When I'm with you I'm so much freer," Sophie adds and pulls a face at the mirror, then sets to work with her brown eye pencil around my eyes. "The biggest, most beautiful eyes in the world. You've got the most perfect almond eyes I've ever seen."

"Abba always said that my cousin Yosseleh who was murdered in the Shoah had eyes exactly like mine," I say.

"Hey, enough now. Look what we're talking about, instead of rehearsing 'Open the gate,'" she chides, wanting to change the subject.

"But I'm pleased and glad that we're able to talk about the most painful, terrible topic we're both linked to through no choice of our own," I say quietly.

"You're my soul sister," Sophie says, hugging me strongly.

"When will we see Sophie and Saraleh? Will we see their airplane? Imma, will they bring Giraffi a friend?"

"We'll see them soon, Yishai." I answer while parking carefully between the lines, which Eddie says is a must in Australia.

EDWARD PERKINS:
23 December 1974

"What? You've swapped your study group for cooking? I don't believe it!" Karl laughed as he helped me peel potatoes for the salad I was making, then shell and chop hard boiled eggs, and crisp gherkins. "Mayo?" he asked.

I knew Sophie loved this kind of potato salad, and Noah taught me how to make it when we were on Shabbat dining hall duty in Kibbutz Ein Yam.

"Focus, Karl, focus," I chuckled. "They'll be here soon."

"And you? Are you focusing? Other than medicine, Talya and Yishai, have you forgotten you're a chess champ?"

"Actually, lately I've started taking part in uni competitions. I hadn't even thought of making time for it because I knew it would be at the expense of the precious little time I have with Talya and Yishai. But about a month ago she took out the chess set her father specially ordered from Krakow for her, and put it in the living room and asked me outright, 'What about your favorite hobby?' Karl, how on earth did I get to the other end of the world and find such a generous spirit who always answers my soul?"

"Well, easy to answer," Karl laughed. "Because of me!

You haven't forgotten, I seriously hope, who urged you to go to Israel!"

"Nope. Haven't forgotten at all."

"Admittedly you've got both the natural talent and the passion for the game but without training you'll soon be facing the limit of your talents and everything will end as nothing. So Talya Karlinski said to me. And she's right as usual," Karl added. "I really hope you'll find the time to get back to it."

"After Talya's put her Dad's set right there in the middle of the dining table I dreamt that I was playing Yosseleh, her cousin, who was the Polish youth champion. Imagine that: he survived almost the entire war, even as far as the Russians' entry into the city, because of this game, because the ghetto deputy commander took care of him for the game's sake. In my dream Yosseleh seemed to be gazing at me through Talya's eyes. Then he spoke to me: 'When I started playing chess, my belief in the mystic powers of a higher divine force began to dissipate.' I asked him why. 'Chess,' he answered, 'is the ultimate marker of the intellect.' And then he disappeared, his smile slowly fading," Eddie said. "My brain got stuck on that sentence for the entire day. I couldn't stop thinking about it."

"Do you know who said what Yosseleh quoted in your dream?"

"No. I was sure it was from him."

"It wasn't," Karl said. "It was Johann Wolfgang von Goethe. So let's sum this up: you'll go back to playing chess and you'll read Goethe."

"Right. Now let's get this salad finished!"

I can hear Sophie's voice back then on the beach. "That's our Talya." Noah stood behind Sophie and smiled in his heart-melting way.

"I'm a bit concerned over the moment that Sophie arrives," I say. "When I was around eight years old, my favorite uncle, my Dad's brother, died in a riding accident. It was my first experience of how death can come in a sudden flash. Dad, Mum and Johnny withdrew, each into their own restrained pain. The house was horribly silent. A paralyzing terror filled me. Maybe that's why I knew from a very young age that I'd become a doctor, working to win at death's game."

Karl was silently thoughtful as he tossed mayonnaise into the bowl.

"Karl, let me finish that. Would you mind setting the table?"

Our preparations done, I poured each of us a beer. We sat down to watch the sun setting over Coogee Beach, with its massive rocks and crannies filled with bright turquoise water. Even though dusk was settling in, the beach was packed with people. Some were already starting to celebrate Christmas with family beachfront picnics. Most were still swimming in that Australian way of laid back enjoyment.

And Karl and I are pleased that everything's ready on time: the table is covered in Talya's favorite purple cloth, the napkins of a lighter lavender are rolled into white napkin rings. The dishes that Talya's father Herman managed to retrieve from Christina's house, who took care of them after Yosseleh's family was forced to move to the ghetto, are now arranged on the table just as Talya likes. The plates are a bright white porcelain and look newly purchased. Each is edged in a fine gold line, next to that is a fine lapis blue line, and on both are the tiniest gold stars.

"When I was little I loved the holidays even more because Abba would agree to use his parents' luxurious dishes but he always warned me about breaking them," Talya told me the first time she hosted Noah and Sophie for a festive dinner.

I remember how she took them gingerly out of the closet and warned me perhaps seven times. "Eddie, be careful not to break them. And stop laughing. Your whole body is shaking and the plates might slip from your hands."

"The perfect table setting," Karl agreed.

Right then Yishai announced their arrival. "We're here! This is our house!" followed by laughter from Saraleh, Sophie and Talya.

Instantly the house fills with happy sounds, colors, scents, hugs, whispered greetings.

Karl hugs her tight. "He'll stay young forever," Sophie whispers into his ear as she wipes a tear away with the back of her hand. They stand that way for what seems a long time.

When Karl lets Sophie go, she hugs me briefly, almost impatiently, and I understand that she needs to regroup inside herself, get back to the practical Sophie we all know. She takes several boxes out of a gray bag and places them on the coffee table.

"Karl, this is from your Papa. I visited Heinrich. He also drove me to the airport." She points to the box covered in paper that shows children in the snow.

"Wow, thanks! I can smell Christmas cake through the wrapping!" Karl smiles and winks as the two share childhood memories.

"Marta absolutely forced me to take these so that Saraleh and Yishai can decorate the Christmas tree," Sophie said, pointing to two pink boxes packed with ornaments.

"Let's take it tomorrow to Eddie's parents. Beth will be pleased," Talya nods.

I know that even though Talya never experienced Christmas, she can feel the pleasant warmth of our memories. One of my earliest is linked to my Mum's chest of drawers. Dad, always busy in the hospital or the clinic, or on a flight to care for the ill on the outback farms, is in charge of bringing the crate of ornaments up from the basement. Mum would let Johnny and I hang the golden balls and red bears on the tree. How carefully we handled them! Two items are in the drawer of the large bureau in Mum's bedroom. She gives one to me and one to Johnny. We know they're very old, from her childhood, and have been passed down from generation to generation. They are crystal balls, and we hang them with great awe. Then Dad hooks the colored lights up, and they reflect gorgeously in the crystals, and we two boys would clap our hands.

Talya takes my hand and leads me towards the kitchen. "Let's get dinner going. Sophie's exhausted."

"I was filled with trepidation over meeting her again."

"I know," Talya says, giving me a quick hug. "Tomorrow or the day after we'll talk about Noah's freckled grin, his big hands, his sheer strength, this stunning love story between a Jewish family from Berlin and the daughter of a Heidelberg SS commander, but for now let's sit down, enjoy the meal, and your wonderful salad."

I kiss her lightly on the lips.

My beloved Talya.

EDWARD PERKINS:
25 – 30 January 1975

Sophie planned on spending several months with us. She might have even planned on staying in Australia for longer, renting a place, trying to rebuild a life alongside her cousin Karl, or near us because we're family. But we're not family. The writing was on the wall. I knew Sophie's father was an SS officer, I knew he loved to play chess: Karl shared those details with me even before I met Talya.

He also said that Sophie left her home at sixteen because she discovered her father was a murderer, and when I listened to stories about Yosseleh, I unconsciously repressed Karl's words. Perhaps I did it consciously, though: perhaps I didn't want to rock the boat and upset this delicate fabric of our love. I never wanted to undermine the relationship with Sophie and Noah. I didn't investigate, I didn't ask where Ludwig Schmidt, who loved chess, was stationed during the war.

During the Holocaust.

During the Shoah.

And this quiet, easy-going country would have been the ideal setting for Talya to have learned that Sophie was the daughter of a sadistic, murdering chess player.

A month after Sophie and Sarah got settled into our home, Talya whispered to me. "I think Sophie feels okay here, almost the way she used to be. Staying with us, and her frequent get-togethers with Karl, are helping her heal. Yesterday she said that Noah was happy she's with us, but this time she didn't cry as she usually does when she talks about him."

"Tomorrow's Friday. I'll take care of the kids. Why don't you go out with Sophie?" I suggested to Talya. "After all, you said that Lily wants to meet with you for brunch at that new café in Double Bay."

"My everlasting love who lives inside my mind and knows my wishes," Talya said, smiling warmly and cuddling up close, then leading me into a waltz spin. How like Talya to do that.

They came back in silence.

Saraleh ran to greet her mother. "Galah! Galah!"

To Sophie's and Talya's puzzled looks Yishai explained that I'd taken the kids to the zoo where we'd seen the fantastic pink birds called galahs, and how much those birds covet shiny objects.

"Sophie, their trainer hides coins and other small shiny things but they always find them!" Yishai added excitedly in his desperate attempt to catch Sophie's attention.

"Come, sweetie," Talya invited Yishai with open arms, "tell me about the zoo."

Sophie picked Sarah up. "I'm going out for a bit of a walk," she said softly.

"What's going on?" I asked when I saw Yishai was concentrating on building castles with Lego that the Perkins grandparents had bought him for Christmas.

Talya, white as the wall of this apartment before we moved in, lowered herself onto the sofa. "There, in Café Marina," she began, tears flowing down her cheeks, "between the laughter and the Eggs Benedict, between the cappuccino, and Lily's 'so glad to meet you at last' and the way Sophie angles her head of curls, this is what Lily said."

Talya took a deep breath and swallowed hard before continuing. "Next week Rabbi Ashenbach, Sydney's Chief Rabbi, will be lecturing to the Shoah studies group at the synagogue. His parents managed to escape to Australia with their five year old son right before the war. They came from a small town near Lublin with the oddest name: Przysucha."

"Lily took an announcement out of her handbag and read it out to us. Here, I have a copy. 'The lecture will focus on the liquidation of the Lublin Ghetto, in which Lublin Jewry was sent to Majdanek, and the 3 November 1943 event in which forty-three thousand Lublin Jews were murdered. This is the largest massacre on one single day during the Shoah. It began at dawn and continued until evening."

She paused and gulped before continuing. "The lecture will take an in-depth look at the Lublin Ghetto Deputy Commander, Commandant Ludwig Schmidt, in charge of ensuring the military operation was fully executed. According to recently discovered documents, he additionally chose the title for the liquidation: Aktion Erntefest, or The Harvest Festival. He managed to evade a court hearing for war criminals, like so many others of the Nazi murderers."

"Then Lily invited us both to attend."

Talya sighed. "Lily said she knows that my father is from Lublin, and how much interest I take in the topic."

I couldn't look into Talya's eyes. I knew what she was thinking. Suddenly everything was abundantly clear.

"How is it you never made that connection?" Talya asked, her lips barely moving. "My super smart Eddie, who notices the most minute of details when it comes to human brain research."

Her voice carried a mix of blame, pain and sarcasm which shocked me. It was the first time I felt that Talya might be capable of breaking her connection with me.

When we first fell in love, after the first time we made love, when I saw the colors weeping from the ceiling, when I heard the music that the massive ficus tree in the kibbutz garden made, when Talya brushed her hair with the purple brush and spoke about Yosseleh and his love of chess, and told me he'd been murdered in the Lublin Ghetto, at that very moment the music stopped, and I understood that it was very possible, in fact probable, that Karl's uncle who loved to play chess in the Lublin Ghetto with a young Jewish teen, was one and the same person, that Karl's and Talya's stories were two sides of the same coin.

I also understood that this flash of comprehension which raced through my mind needed to evaporate, and never be worded by my lips, because what I wanted most was to hear the music that Talya and I made, to make Talya my wife and life.

A mistake.

But how could I tell her, back then, what my flash of a thought was! Talya hasn't spoken to me now for a week.

SOPHIE SCHMIDT
25 January 1975

"I knew it," I said when we left the café in Double Bay. A heavy silence filled the car. I could see Talya's profile, her lips pursed tight, her hands gripping the wheel so hard that the veins on the backs of her hands stood out. I'd waited years for this moment. It arrived without prior warning but the relief was instant. I spoke in an easy flow.

"When I was in Heidelberg before your marriage, Mama gave me letters that Ludwig wrote to her from Lublin. I realized that he was the ghetto deputy. I also read about the Jewish boy who played chess with him. He described how he kept that boy alive in the Lublin Fortress despite most of the Jews having already been killed."

"But I was too afraid to tell you before the wedding. Then I repeatedly put it off, and then you came here with Eddie and you were dealing with adjusting here, and then Noah was killed, and along with him went the inner voice that kept saying 'Sophie, you've got to tell Talya. Sophie, you must tell Talya. Sophie....'"

And then I broke into tears. And couldn't calm down. Talya stopped the car and passed me a bottle of water. Deep in my heart, I hoped she'd hug me. No hug was forthcoming.

"What I fear most, Talya, is losing people close to me. At sixteen I underwent major surgery, let's call it, and was left emotionally brutalized. But because of Frau Eisenberg, and Noah, and you, Talya, especially you, I got through it. I lost my history teacher. I've lost Noah. I'm so scared to lose you too, Talya."

Talya was silent, biting her lower lip. A gesture I know so well. Her eyes are dry.

"How could you, Sophie? Did you get dressed up? Did you choose a costume in the Nazi basement? Did you dress up as a good German who understands the enormity of the crimes? How could you have hidden the connection that your father, who you yourself label a murderer, had to Yosseleh?"

I see that her lower lip has a drop of blood on it. She's bitten through it. She breathes deeply. I can see she's doing her utmost to keep herself in check.

"We can't be people who love you anymore. We aren't your family anymore," she blurts.

She turns the key in the ignition switch and we drive in absolute silence to the house in Coogee Beach. We go in. Saraleh runs towards me. Yishai is bubbling with the news that they were at the zoo.

TALYA KARLINSKY
31 January 1975

I watch the malady creeping into my veins, my arteries, my capillaries, from the tips of my toes to the crown of my head. I'm a tree with black, rotten branches.

"She's got a high fever," I can hear Eddie saying. "She might have caught something at the café."

"I don't understand why Sophie flew back so suddenly," I hear Beth remarking.

Voices grow louder. Voices distance.

Abba-Herman appears. His face is right up close to mine. His blue eyes smile at me reassuringly. "Sweetheart, you need to rest. You'll be well again soon."

He always asked if I'd rested enough and I always hated the question: what's all this about resting? I've got so much to do! But now I love him for that question. It makes me happy. I hug him hard. He dissipates.

"Eddie," I whisper. "Eddie."

"I'm here, right with you, sweetheart. I'm so glad you're awake."

"Yishai?"

"He's in kindergarten. Beth collects him every day. She's taken a place in Vaucluse near Parsley Bay. She wants to help. Dr. Russell can handle his patients perfectly fine and is probably secretly happy that he's got a bit of a reprieve from her constant concern about his diabetes," Eddie chuckled.

I'm not angry with Eddie. The anger's gone. The heavy cloud that fogged every cell in my body is begging to lift skywards and disappear. I vow to do everything possible so that

Eddie can realize his dream
and complete his studies
and research
and discover
and help people
and love, the way only he can.

His face is next to mine. His scent penetrates my body, mingles with the blood and plasma and saliva and hair. We become one.

Yosseleh hovers above me, and his face keeps alternating with Eddie's.

"What is it, Talya?" Eddie asks softly, with his brown eyes, their thick rim of eyelashes. He studies me with a worried look. The boy from Lublin has turned into the boy from Melbourne, passing through my mind, my thoughts, shaking my soul to its core.

"How long have I been lying here?"

"Five days. You had a really high temperature."

"I never have fever."

"Sweetheart," he whispers, as his babyface comes closer.

"I'm fine," I sit up. "Help me get to the shower?"

Eddie shampoos my hair. Eucalyptus scent fills the bathroom. He washes my shoulders, my back, my arms, and steps out of the shower. My man. So manly.

So considerate. I step out too, my arms held wide. He embraces me.

"I'm going to make you a decent breakfast. The kind you love: scrambled eggs, salad chopped in tiny-tiny pieces the way they do on kibbutz, with lots of tahini. I found a Greek store nearby that has fabulous tahini. The best, like home!"

"And a cup of tea?"

"With a slice of lemon. Sure," he smiles at me.

He puts Schubert's Serenade, the one I love, on the record player and heads for the kitchen while I sit in an armchair facing the beach and ponder the essence of love. I think about the color red. And the flash that lights Edward Perkins' eyes when he gazes at me in our special moments.

Is that what I was considering foregoing? What luck I had that my body decided to collapse when I got too furious and frustrated at the image of Sophie's father standing over Yosseleh with his whip passing through my mind's eye. The tears I begin to shed are such a relief. What's come over me? What am I: some kind of self-righteous examiner of other people's hearts and souls? Who knows what Eddie experienced when he suppressed the story.

One thing became very clear, though: Eddie had only been trying to protect our love. At the relationship's start I felt that his love was driven by passion. I was in more of a wary, analytical frame of mind, more passive. Slowly I began to feel an ecstasy from discovering that nothing is more arousing and pleasurable and poetic and musical and clear and fulfilling than that deep love. A love that was confident, evident, the kind where I knew I cared even about the nail of his small toe, and where he cared about the way I almost choked every time I felt extremely tense or pressured.

I'd never enjoyed a breakfast as much as I did that morning in our Coogee Beach home.

"So how's the tahini?" he grinned. "Like on kibbutz, right?"

I swallowed another mouthful, took a long sip of tea, and covered Eddie's face with tiny kisses: the dimple on his right cheek, the tip of his nose, the lids of his eyes. It was a quick, easy decision to take.

Luckily, I was still on the long summer school vacation. I spent the days shaping a second childhood together with Yishai. The Nutcracker Suite, Swan Lake, Peter Pan: we took in show after show, put on for the Christmas holidays in the stunning new Opera House on the harbor, inaugurated a year earlier, just around when we arrived. Watching Yishai, who could sing before he could talk, absorbing the music, and listening to him talk about the plots and ask pertinent questions, made my heart leap with joy and soothed my spirit. And that led me to feeling that the way Sophie and I broke off from each other, and the shock that caused me a complete internal upheaval, was slowly evaporating, too.

"When will Saraleh come back?" Yishai asked after the little girl and her mother had returned to Israel.

Oddly, he asked Eddie, not me. Eddie always gave the same answer. "Australia is very far away. A trip needs a lot of planning. But if you like, we can write her a letter."

Four times he asked, and then stopped.

"Talya, don't worry. Yishai has a very full life. It's part

of the separation process," Eddie reassured. My guy, for whom my feelings and thoughts are an open book.

I made sure Eddie had the time he needed to delve into his studies, as well as a course of special interest: circadian clocks. He explained that a field of brain research examined the link between our biological clocks and our genetics, and that many of our psychological processes have a daily rhythm.

"Current research is studying this interconnection, which until now had been a complete mystery despite the huge advances in brain research," Eddie said.

"How can that be examined?"

"Using data on changes in the zebra fish's behavior, the first living creature on which genetic engineering caused changes to its traits. These studies might give us insight on how circadian genes impact our brains."

"Then maybe you can reach conclusions on the biggest question there is: if there's a certain gene that boosts the tendency to pure evil in a specific individual?"

Eddie clutched me and spun me around in our funny dizzy dance and began singing a silly song he made up when we first fell in love in Kibbutz Ein Yam.

"A guy from Australia, fell in love with Talya, because…"

Then he waited expectantly for my answer.

"Because Talya is a medal-yeah!"

He doesn't stop spinning us both around until I answer! We fall back on the bed laughing our heads off. He gazed at me.

"That's exactly my goal for my med degree and the research I'm planning: to reach conclusions about its link to Syndrome E. The syndrome of evil."

"Go, go, off to your studies with you!' I shoo him away playfully. "I'm off to bring Yishai from the neighbor. She's got a Pomeranian called Tasmania that he's crazy about."

TALYA KARLINSKI
end July 1985

Givatayim. We'll go there from Sydney. I'll take Eddie back to my childhood haunts. Who is this Eddie of mine? The time's come to talk about him, understand his complex personality, and the privilege of living with his wonderful nature.

Eddie is the outcome of careful Anglo-Saxon education, a gentleman, from crown to toe, a phrase I love from Shakespeare's Macbeth. When he'd open the door to the battered jeep used in the cotton fields, which he'd drive from kibbutz to buy me felafel from the old-timers in Haifa's lower town, Sophie always burst into laughter.

"I need to get Noah's down-to-earth Israeli nature more like that," she'd say. "He doesn't seem to understand what I'm talking about when I ask him not to walk so fast ahead of me on our way to the kibbutz dining hall, and he'd never open the car door. Look what a door-opening gem you landed!"

"Nor does it upset a single teensy feminist cell in my entire body," I laughed, too. "On the contrary! I'm actually familiar with it and love it. It's just how Herman behaved."

"So your Abba took you on walks from his place in

Tel Aviv a couple of streets from the beach to the shore via Allenby Street?" Eddie asked after I'd told him how much Abba had loved swimming in the sea and walking along Tel Aviv's streets, which he once said reminded him quite a bit of Lublin even though, on the other hand, they were completely dissimilar.

In summer, after we'd spent time at the beach, where I'd spread Velveta on his slightly sunburnt shoulders, there was a sentence he'd repeat. "Talinka, in Poland there were forests and rivers. That's where we spent our fun time as kids."

Of course Eddie remembered me telling him those details on some occasion. One day Eddie returned in the afternoon, red-faced and sweating. I knew he'd gone to the Australian Embassy in Tel Aviv to extend his passport's validity.

"I took your Abba's route. I went from Gruzenberg Street to Allenby Street and from there to the sea. I passed the stores you told me about: Metzkin Ivanir the photographer, where the front window was full of photos of all the VIPs where you'd stop to gaze and your father would always say, 'Talinka, c'mon, let's keep moving.' I also peeked into Nahalat Binyamin Street and the store called Salpeter Furs where Herman worked. I reached the Opera House and turned right into Hayarkon Street and sat on a bench there drinking freshly pressed juice and gazing at the sea."

I laughed so much that I almost choked. "Well, just who are you, Edward Perkins? Which planet did you come from?"

He hugged me tight. I could smell his sweaty body.

Normally he never smelled like that.

"I love you so much," he said softly, getting down on one knee and taking a ring from his pocket. "I bought this in Allenby because I remembered you said there were a whole bunch of jewelry stores there. I want to breathe the air you breathe, and smell your hair all my life."

It was a year since we'd met, and Eddie proposed.

"Did you go from Gruzenberg to the beach?" I asked, after telling him to get up. Eddie blushed and stood, smiling in his heart-melting, slightly bashful way.

"But say yes. Yes!" his eyes locked on mine.

I loved him so much, I loved how different he was, I loved his manner, and the way he didn't try at all to change into someone else. I loved his mind. I loved his body, which was a mingling of robust and relaxed. I loved the spark in his eyes.

"Yes. Yes," I said. "We'll live in Ein Yam."

"We'll live wherever you like," Eddie answered.

And Eddie did not confirm his acceptance into Sydney University until I said that I was ready to move to Australia. Now he had just accepted an offer to head the brain research laboratory, or more precisely, to establish it, as part of the Life Sciences Faculty at Tel Aviv University.

"We'll live in Givatayim," I said happily.

"Wherever you wish," Professor Edward Perkins-Karlinski grinned at me.

I was so moved when, on receiving his Professorship, he said that if I was agreeable to the idea, he'd be honored to bear my family name as a mark of respect. Then he proceeded to have all his official documents altered accordingly.

"Eddie, Eddie," I danced around him, "how did you think of finding work in the university I love so much?"

"Talya, during your years of study while we lived in Ein Yam you never stopped talking about Professor Yabetz, head of the history department and an expert in Roman history who'd joke that Latin's compulsory because it's like Yiddish. Because of him, and after hearing your stories about Yosseleh and how much Yiddish was loved in your home, you specialized in Shoah studies."

"Yes, true," I agreed. "He released me from serving as his personal assistant and sent me off to Professor Bauer. And he was right, of course. I don't think I'll ever get Yosseleh out of my system for as long as I live. For me, the way to honor him is to constantly study the Shoah."

Luckily for me, the University of New South Wales had a department in its faculty of education which developed syllabus content. I'd proposed at the time to my doctoral advisor that my dissertation delve into ways to teach about the Holocaust in high schools. The idea was considered innovative. In Australia until then, history lessons taught about WWII but the Holocaust earned no more than a mere mention, and certainly no in-depth study. Of course my inspiration for framing the syllabus developed while I taught at the Jewish day school in Sydney. The Professor consulted with his colleagues for a week, then contacted me with news that I could go ahead.

"There's a chance that Talya will alter the entire Australian education system," I heard Eddie at the time say in his understated manner to Beth.

I was so thrilled that Eddie would now be holding a

leading position in Tel Aviv University, where my own life had been so significantly shaped.

"Rona wrote that the house where her Aunt Trudie, who lived in the neighborhood where we used to play together, and slide down the dunes, is up for sale. We used to think it was such a mountain, but it's really no more than a hilltop. Her aunt used to tell us to look at the wild crocuses and snowbells on the hill. Her eyes lit up with wonder when she spoke about them, and that was long before a law was passed prohibiting wildflowers from being picked. I tried to convince Rona to dig one or two out with their bulbs and replant them in the garden of where I lived in Givatayim but Rona was not having any of that. 'You're afraid of your aunt!' I remember taunting her."

"And she had a simple answer. 'I am, and she's right.' Rona was much closer to her Aunt Trudie than to her parents. She's the sole inheritor of that house, Eddie. She said she has no problem waiting for us to return and then we can discuss buying it. She'll never abandon her socialist Ein Yam dream."

Eddie's thoughtful gaze was directed at me. "Alright, we'll get all our meager resources together and make the effort, on condition that you promise to make me compote very often."

How can anyone not laugh at, and agree to, that? "I promise. I promise. So you want to go back to Rosa's kindergarten?"

"Only if you come with me," he said, hugging me. "What luck I found you. Who else could understand how much I love those old-time Jewish foods that Rosa fed us."

"But what's so important about the compote?" I asked the question that would trigger a wave of laughs.

"Because it's good for the metabolism!" we answered simultaneously, falling back on the bed in peals of laughter, and he kissed me the way he used to, and we made love the way we used to, before our thoughts were so busy with studies and work and life-changing decisions. And right at the moment when I wanted him so badly, he was there, inside me. And I floated higher and higher.

"That's how we feel when we're living. That's how we beat death," Eddie whispered in my ear as I curled up into my special spot against his body which always soothed the storm.

We lay in silence.

"Yishai will be home soon from school," I said. "That's my real worry. How will he, a young teen and so entrenched in the Ozzie culture, integrate with his peers in Israel."

"Well, music is his anchor. Being accepted to the Thelma Yellin National School of Arts provides a solid foundation. Musicians have a universal but uniquely shared language. I think it won't be the easiest thing for him initially but don't forget, he's your son…" Eddie's words were comforting. "And the school's only a few streets away from where we'll live. Could you ask any better than that?"

Stroking my cheek, Eddie gave that smile of his that always made me feel everything would be safe.

SOPHIE SCHMIDT
9 November 1989

I watch them climbing the wall and jumping off its rim. I see the hugs and tears and joy in their eyes. The Berlin Wall has fallen.

I can't but help think about Talya who's probably sitting with Eddie, both of them glued to the TV, tears of happiness in their eyes. But why can't my life carry on without that shadow of separation?

Seated in the brown armchair that Talya and Eddie gave me before they flew to Australia, my head's spinning. These are the most amazing images of our lifetime. The moment seventeen years ago when I landed in Sydney, the hugs, the tears, the walks along Coogee Beach, the Christmas meals with Karl. Yishai's and Saraleh's laughter and the way they played together. The feeling of warmth and the knowledge that Noah is experiencing it all along with us.

The love.

Like a choking gob of phlegm, the feeling of terrible loss rose in my chest. If only I'd told Talya about Ludwig Schmidt shortly after meeting her, I wouldn't have lost her. That drive back from the Double Bay café when Lily invited us to the lecture on Lublin, the Jews of which were almost completely eradicated, and the discovery that my father had been the Lublin Ghetto's deputy commander, made Talya say what I've never forgotten all these years: "You're the one dressed up as a good German."

Her words pierced and rocked my soul, and brought me back onto the real track of my life. Shortly after leaving Australia and returning to kibbutz, I asked the kibbutz committee to approve the budget needed to study social work. I, Sophie Schmidt, daughter of a mass murderer, who rebelled in adolescence, left a warm home because I no longer felt I belonged there.

But I never fully realized the scope of the task I needed to take on to truly belong.

Once I was back at Kibbutz Ein Yam, I moved smoothly into the Israel life and routine. A normal life. A life of love with Noah. I became Sophie Mendelsohn. I became an IDF widow. I became the mother of Sarah. Yes, I was sort of living under the guise of "the good German," but the visit to Talya in Australia tore my mask off.

"She actually did you a huge favor," Noah spirits his logic to me. He'd appear every day. He'd appear back then almost every hour. He'd talk to me through my thoughts as I sat in the brown armchair. "She set you back on your destiny. After all, in the first conversation you and I had in Berlin, you spoke about helping Shoah survivors. You spoke about how that would be a very suitable role, in light of being born to a Holocaust murderer, the man who organized the massacre of the Lublin Ghetto Jews, labeling it a harvesting."

My beloved Noah has been reading my mind for seventeen years now. I felt tremendous relief when the kibbutz committee authorized my studies. Rona came over to shake my hand.

"I'm sure you'll do a really good job," she said in her practical manner that always made Talya laugh whenever she spoke about her long-time school friend from Givatayim, and their activities in the Hashomer Hatza'ir youth movement.

Rona was right. My life is dedicated to assisting those who, in my thoughts, I call trees without branches and leaves. It took years for Israel's government to understand that beyond the Shoah survivors' health and physical disabilities, many also bore extremely complex psychological damage.

For my master's degree research I interviewed hundreds of Shoah survivors. They spoke of the long silence they were made to bear, or which they forced onto themselves. Many said that silence was the only defense mechanism they could use to avoid re-experiencing the events and humiliation they underwent. They were hesitant about disclosing their weaknesses, feeling that no one really wanted to listen to them.

A sentence recurred in many interviews. "Israel was busy with existential wars after achieving independence. The wars led to new suffering, so who had the patience for our stories…" Words of sorrow. Words accompanied by strong feeling of guilt for not having risen up and done something. Words of understanding in retrospect that no country, in fact, possessed the knowledge of how to aid survivors of a genocide of such scope.

For years now I've served as psychological consultant and manager of the Haifa Psychiatric Clinic, which cares for Shoah survivors who, as time passes and their age advances, suffer even greater distress. I listen to their voices. I talk the language of their childhoods and youth. I organize groups of German volunteers to work with them.

Rona was the first to request that I tell my own story during a conference held after Yom Hashoah on Kibbutz Ein Yam. In all honesty, I was very hesitant to agree. I also remembered Talya's words about her childhood friend. "Beneath Rona's tough outer shell is an amazingly delicate and understanding soul."

"But, Imma," Sarah said to me, "your story is unique and it will also help you answer the question of identity that you keep agonizing over: as the daughter of a Nazi murderer, who are you?"

My daughter, who never hesitates to state her thoughts pointedly and smartly.

And so I began to talk about my personal history in lectures on kibbutz, in schools, in seminars throughout Israel. The burdensome clutch on my being slowly began lifting from my shoulders.

On Yom Kippur and on the day before any of the numerous Jewish festivals begin, many of my patients know I'll be in the clinic if needed. I have a room there and often sleep over.

"Excited about the Berlin Wall coming down?" I hear Noah.

"I have to renew my connection with Talya. It's the first time since we broke contact that I feel an urgent need to be in touch with her," I tell him. And as I speak, I notice it was also the first time I wasn't on the verge of tears thinking about it.

"You're realizing your life's purpose. Helping Shoah survivors. I remember how amazed I was at your confidence and determination in your first interview with me in Berlin," Noah says softly. "Don't be afraid. Write to her."

He gave his feline grin, the one that reminded me of Alice in Wonderland, and faded away.

I'll write to Talya, saying that even though I was born into the Schmidt family of Heidelberg, I'm Sophie of Kibbutz Ein Yam, a social worker assisting Shoah survivors to the best of my capability.

I imagine Ludwig playing chess with that beautiful boy in the photo, in his sweater with holes in its sleeves, and his clever mind showing in his eyes: the boy named Yosseleh Zilberman-Karlinski who is your cousin, Talya.

I can't atone for the horrors which my parents and my people enacted against your people, but every day I try to help those who survived cope with their lives, their memories, their pain and loss. I see them. I listen to their stories. I hear the stories from the few who survived the Lublin Ghetto liquidation about the horrors of the Erntefest, the Fortress, Majdanek, and I hear them talk about Ludwig Schmidt.

I am conducting thorough research on the Germans' meticulous plans to ethnically cleanse Jews from Germany and all Europe.

A strange tranquility begins to settle around me.

I know that the people thrashing at the wall with sledgehammers have nothing to do with me.

EDWARD PERKINS
9 November 1989

The phone rings.
"Are you watching history happen before your eyes or have you got your head stuck in some article about satanic brain function in humans?"

It's Karl and his voice carries its usual touch of sarcasm which, when our friendship first began to take shape, annoyed me but now makes me feel almost as close to him as a brother.

"You understand that this is one of the most important events of the second half of our crazy twentieth century? I wish I could come over and watch it together with you.

I laugh. "Talya's already called me a few times to come and watch it. A few moments and I'll be done with the article I actually am stuck in and I'll join her and Yishai. How're things doing in the Heidelberg branch of the Deutsche Bank's investment department?"

"You won't believe this but I'm starting my doctorate in German history. Like Talya always said when we were all together in Australia, 'People, the human psyche, that's the pivot of life.' The numbers are fine but bottom line, they do get boring. I ridiculed the notion at the time.

Now, at my somewhat more advanced age, I must say that Mrs. Perkins Karlinski was totally right."

"Well, I bet I don't need to guess your dissertation topic."

"We'll talk about it some other time. Go and watch how the people of East Germany are smashing that wall away!"

A shudder of acknowledgment runs through me, as it frequently has over the past. If not for Karl popping up in my life when we were both young students in Sydney, I'd never have met Talya, and probably never have become Edward Perkins-Karlinski, the researcher studying what makes regular folk into cold-blooded murderers.

Professor Fried came to mind. "Let me tell you a story," I remember him telling me following his lecture on the findings of dissected brains taken from 'ordinary' murderers. This was during my last year of specialization in neurosurgery at Sydney University.

"It was in Berlin. 1938," the Professor continued. "My father, Dr. Jozef Fried, was an active Zionist who lectured in synagogues in Berlin, trying to convince Jews to emigrate to the Land of Israel as the signs of social deterioration were becoming increasingly evident. One day after his talk, a certain man wearing a very elegant coat came up to him. 'Herr Doktor,' he spoke very politely. 'Can you explain the difference between the Babylonian Talmud and the Jerusalem Talmud?' So my father explained in detail."

"The two men, so my father described, stood so close to each other that their white puffs of breath mingled. Who could ever have imagined that one of the two would shortly turn into a blood-thirsty monster? The man asking the questions presented himself as Adolf Eichmann. I believe," the Professor said, looking at me, "it was that exchange which roused my interest in the sources of human evil."

Right then I recalled the first time I asked Talya what had happened to her cousin. Very quickly after she discovered how much I loved chess, she told me the story about his genius for the game. When he'd been a mere five years old, he'd seen two children beating another very young child in Gesia Street. Rabbi Karlinski shooed the older children away and took the littler one into the house. It was then that Yosseleh had said he wants to study why there are people who really enjoy being bad, and he wants to find out how to heal them.

"What made you decide it was the field you wanted to specialize in?" I heard the Professor asking.

I, Edward Perkins, an Australian child, who grew up sailing on the Yarra River and swimming in St. Kilda, reciting the poetry of Yeats and hearing his mother's cello playing, flew with his surgeon father to outback areas where he cared for the ill Aborigine populations, when did I know that I wanted to study and research the part of the human brain responsible for the ultimate form of evil?

"Ludwig Schmidt, Deputy Commander at the Lublin Ghetto, who played chess against my wife Talya's young cousin, and who labeled the ghetto's liquidation 'Erntenfest,' was what drove me towards this field," I answered.

The Professor's face showed no surprise at all.

"When you get to Israel, contact me," he nodded and warmly shook my hand.

"You're missing the greatest show ever. The Berlin Wall's coming down." I can hear my love, Talya, calling out.

"Coming," I call out in answer. "Where's Yishai?"

"You were concentrating so much on your call that you didn't hear him tell you he's heading out for a rehearsal with Givatayim's Chamber Orchestra at Founders' House."

I sigh. "Without the guilt trip, please…" I sort of plead in a little voice.

"So many years and you're still such a sweetie," Talya says, amused.

I sit on the blue velour sofa next to her, my arm around her shoulders. She snuggles up close.

"I've been thinking about my chat with Professor Fried. Was the start of my interest in the human brain really Ludwig Schmidt, or…"

"Rosa's kindergarten," Talya interrupts, "or the Bar Mitzvah day when Rosa had you listen to the start of the Eichmann Trial, or us falling in love, or… what difference does it make? Do you remember what you said after your first year of studies in Sydney?"

"Yes. That I want to research the brains of regular folk who love toast and coffee in the morning, listen with moist eyes to Mendelsohn's violin concerto, write love letters to a future spouse, and in the evening turn into mass murderers."

"And you also said that you have no interest in serial murderers, whose violent minds have been studied for years already."

Talya gazes at me with her big almond-shaped eyes, and I know that only because of her, I've achieved my ambitions.

"How about giving me a bit of reflexology with your piano fingers and together we'll watch how the children of those Nazis, may their names be erased for all time, smash the wall to bits," she chuckles, lying down on the sofa and swinging her feet up and onto my lap.

"We'll invite Sophie and Saraleh to your lecture in Lublin. It's a good place and time to restore bidirectional family relations between murderer and murdered," she says, laughing again but this time it turns into the familiar cough that whelms her in moments of tension.

"Excellent plan," I say, smiling as I go to the kitchen to bring Talya a glass of water with a slice of fresh lemon.

TALYA KARLINSKI
9 November 1989

I watch them climbing the wall and jumping down, I watch the embraces, the tears, the smiles, the trembling. Berlin Wall is crashing down. People are taking its stones as souvenirs. For sure she's also sitting glued to her TV with tears in her eyes. But why can't my life go on without the shadow of Sophie hovering around all these years?

People leave each other during their lives and each goes their own way. Sophie isn't a friend from my childhood, my teen years, the youth movement, or from Israel. She's from Germany, land of willing genocidists.

"Phone her," Eddie says, as though reading my thoughts.

"I've read studies on separation. Eddie, did you know it takes a person an average of eighteen months to get over the loss of someone they loved? But I didn't find any statistics about the loss of a German friend whose life intertwined with a Jewish and Israeli friend for quite a few years. Separation is part of the journey of life, though, is it not, Dr. Perkins?"

"Phone her," Eddie repeats softly. "She's probably scared out of her wits to initiate the first contact."

His long fingers gently stroke my hands. "Look how

thrilled those people are, crossing the wall. Their human spirit is free at last."

Indeed the scenes playing out on TV are fascinating. Yishai, soon to enlist in the army, walks in. Tall, slim, good looking, with a smile that from the distance instantly reminds people of his father's, but from up close is clearly different. It's not the Edward Perkins smile that confidently says, "Here I am." Yishai's smile brings to mind testing the water in the bath. When he was a baby, I'd test the bathwater with a finger. When I was sure it was that perfect pleasantness, I'd lower him into the water gingerly, and a smile would very slowly, almost gingerly, spread across his face until his huge brown almond-shaped eyes, ringed in thick eyelashes, would smile too.

Yishai and I went out to the balcony. We stood in a favorite spot from where we could see Tel Aviv's city lights sparkling.

"Givat Kozlovsky is such an incredible location," Yishai nodded.

When Rona and I were little girls we visited her Aunt Trudie and I remember saying almost the same thing. "Tel Aviv's lights are like a great big jewelry box." Every time we visited Rona's aunt after that, we'd all say, "Let's look at the jewel-box," and giggle. Of course I told Eddie and Yishai that story. Now they'll often say "Let's take a look at Imma's jewel-box" when we step out to the balcony. It gives me a warm fuzzy feeling. So there we are, the three of us, arm in arm, watching the lights dance around the city.

Yishai managed to surprise his very optimistic Abba with how quickly and smoothly he integrated into Israeli society. In no time he became part of the Thelma Yellin music scene.

"Well, insisting back in Australia that I keep talking Hebrew, read Hebrew books, and sending me to the Jewish day school even though I protested, if I remember rightly, made it a whole lot easier for me here," Yishai said in one of our balcony chats. He kissed my cheek. That made my eyes well up.

Being fluent in both languages made Yishai even more popular among his friends because he was always ready to help them with their English language subjects.

At the school's year-end concert, after the chamber orchestra played Dvorjak's "American" String Quartet No.12, the music studies coordinator made a brief announcement.

"The next piece is titled 'Lowest Place on Earth' and was written by one of our music students who, I'm pleased to add, has just been accepted into the IDF Music Excellence track. Yishai Perkins-Karlinski."

I squeeze Eddie's hand as he tries to shake it free and applause the fantastic news. Yishai goes on stage, bows to the audience, and sits at the piano with that small smile of his. Ayala, a classmate, comes on stage with her cello to accompany him.

"I thought it was a piano sonata," I whisper.

"How could 'The Lowest Place on Earth' not include a cello?" Eddie whispers back.

I know that Yishai's composition was inspired by visits to his grandmother Dina, who went to live in the desert city of Arad in southern Israel after spending fifteen years in America. She left her American husband, was about to return to Israel, and a week prior to the date set for departure, met her third husband in New York when he visited the Upper East Side Jewish community of Bnei Yeshurun to lecture about his new book, 'The History of the Menorah.' It delved into the background of the massive seven-branched candelabra which is Israel's national symbol, based on the ancient menorah of the two Biblical temples. Dina had gone up to the book's author after the talk and their conversation just took off as though they were long-time friends.

On the evening that Dina advised she was returning, Eddie and I lay in bed. He kissed my eyes and the tip of my nose, and ran his fingers softly through my hair.

"The crisis you experienced when she left Herman is clear, but the time's come to let go of that, my sweet Talya. The true art of our lives is not in constantly trying to be rid of the problems and difficulties but live comfortably alongside them. We're getting older, and she's already old, and she does love you. It's time to reconcile."

I curled up in my special spot against his body. I needed those wise words. From the moment she returned to Israel, perhaps because of her devotion and love for Yishai, perhaps because of Eddie's influence, I rediscovered my mother Dina.

"Why'd you give your composition that title?" I asked Yishai later when we stood together on the balcony watching Tel Aviv's lights.

"Well, because Savta Dina said that after the war, when she and Saba Herman took the train from Tashkent to Warsaw, she got off the train in her grandmother's town, Sarny, and walked to where the house stood. She remembered it always smelling of the special foods made for Shabbat, and for Jewish festivals. It was where all the family gathered, and sat together around the table in the kitchen.

"Savta Dina said that she found Fyodor, the non-Jewish helper, there. He described how all the town's Jews were marched into the nearby forest where she used to enjoy bonfires with fellow members of the Jewish Hashomer Hatza'ir youth movement, where the Jewish Scouts would hold camps for their young members, where she first kissed her young boyfriend from the youth movement. In that forest, her grandmother and her uncles and aunts and cousins and neighbors and teachers dug great pits, and when they were done, the Germans and Ukrainians made them stand in the pits and shot them."

"Fyodor told her that they also shot Savta Dina's mother, who refused to get on the horse-drawn wagon that the school principal lent Dina to help her mother, her little sister and herself flee to Russia. Fyodor said that Savta Dina's grandfather refused to walk to the forest so he was shot right there in the street. 'He's buried here under the fir tree,' Fyodor told her, 'and now get out because this house is mine.' Saba Herman grabbed her by the arm. 'Let's go before they kill us!' he'd said as he pulled her quickly away."

"Savta Dina said she was so furious that she was ready to smash Fyodor's face, but Herman saved her. They hurried to the train station and there, heard about the horrific murders of Jews who came back seeking their homes only to face all the 'Fyodors,' so to speak, who'd simply taken what was not theirs to take."

As Yishai spoke, his eyes filled with tears. "She said," he continued, "that she told herself she was clearly in the lowest place on earth, and from there she could only rise up."

Like a child, I waited expectantly for Yishai to continue. There was a lengthy silence. And then I heard Eddie.

"She saw the world. She worked in a field she loved, education and teaching, and suddenly found herself right by the Dead Sea, the lowest place on earth, but in this case, one that makes her feel tranquil and serene."

"I'd never heard that story," I said, tearing up. Eddie stroked my hair.

"You were so busy listening to Saba Herman's stories and consoling him. There's no need to feel guilty about it. No one can absorb everything, and certainly not in the fierce way you do," Eddie said.

"But your mother lives in Israel now. Maybe try to spend a bit more time with her," Yishai suggested softly.

Once again that choking feeling surfaced, that lump which seems to block my airpipe.

I stepped back indoors, recalling Eddie's and my first vacation together at the Lot Hotel on the Dead Sea's shores. I'd gone out for a 6 am walk, and didn't wake Eddie. The Dead Sea's heat wasn't evident yet at that early hour and the wind lifted and lowered my hair like a bridal veil. Not far along, I sat on one of the chairs scattered around and listened to the water's murmur. The sun seemed to rise all at once, breaking into gold over the sea. The word surfacing in my mind was "genesis," just like in the Picture Book Bible I used to love so much as a very young child.

I turned to Eddie, slipping my feet into the pink New

Balance shoes I loved so much and which I bought in a Coogee sports store. "I'm going for a walk," is all I said.

Yes, my two men are right, I nodded in agreement with my thoughts. The time's come for some balance with my own Imma. And the time's come to renew the connection with Sophie.

SOPHIE SCHMIDT
February 1990

I read the invitation at least five times. I couldn't stop trembling. The invitation contained two printed images: one was Professor Edward Perkins-Karlinski in his Tel Aviv University office, surrounded by shelves literally groaning with books, smiling in that way that goes right to a person's heart. It was the smile Noah loved so much.

"What a winner smile that Australian's got," Noah had whispered in my ear when we sat on the beachfront after the banana picking team had been organized. It had been the night I introduced Eddie to Talya.

And the second image was a family photo, probably in Yarkon Park in central Tel Aviv. Talya sat on a bench, Eddie stood behind her, his pianist hands resting on her shoulders. Yishai stood next to his Abba, tall, straight backed, and very handsome. Yishai and Talya had a more serious look on their faces. Eddie of course wore his usual wonderful smile.

Talya's hair, which once had been such a source of envy for me, especially when my curls went wild if not blow-dried after being shampooed, was still long, straight, hanging down both sides of her face, accentuating her wonderful cheekbones and those huge almond shaped eyes. She was wearing a white top of the kind she always loved, and black, tailored pants. On the middle finger of her hand was the ever-present turquoise ring.

Beneath the photos was the text, printed in cursive script:

You are cordially invited to a lecture
by Professor Edward Perkins-Karlinski,
internationally renowned brain researcher, on:
Becoming a Mass Murderer: Syndrome E,
the biologically driven force
behind human evil.

I note that the lecture will be held in Catholic University, Lublin, Poland. I see Talya's face and hear her voice clearly in my mind. "Not a day of my life went by that I didn't think of you. I knew the day would come when I'd want us to be in touch again. Life's a Sisyphean trip, Sophie. Every day I picked my rock up and suddenly I froze. Our love for each other hovered above me, refusing to let me forget. I see your tears starting to flow and mingling with mine."

"That's our Talya for sure," Noah whispers into my thoughts. "You waited seventeen years for a sign of life from her. Not a day went by that you didn't think of her, too. It's very like Talya to close one circle and open another by positioning both of you where the events that connected you actually took place, separated the two of you, and now bring you back together."

"Yes," I whispered to Noah. "The place where my sadist father abused and murdered her young cousin."

"And the rest of her family, and thousands of Jews more, as you learned." Noah fades away.

His brown armchair is still at the same angle it always was in the living room. How he loved that chair. And now Saraleh is back. Ein Yam is no longer the only kibbutz in the area. Several more were established in the past few years, and she studies at what's now the regional school.

"What's up, Mami?" she asks, studying me with those 'never miss a thing' eyes she inherited from her Abba. She comes over and bobs down. I hug her and wordlessly hold the invitation out.

"At last," Saraleh says. "I've heard about Talya and Eddie my whole life, about the visit to Australia, about Yishai playing with me when we were babies. You always said they're your lost family. When I asked what happened you always got teary-eyed and that scared me so much that I stopped asking. I do know that they were on the kibbutz. Matan said that his mother Rona is still in touch with Talya."

"I'm so sorry about the whole thing," I sighed, "but we'll go to Lublin and there we'll tell our story, okay, sweetie?"

Saraleh didn't answer. All I could do was hug her close.

"And there in Poland we'll go back to being a family," I tried to reassure us both.

"I'm going to study for the history test with Matan," she said. "Will you be okay?"

"Yes, go, go on," I smiled at her. She'd made me so happy when, three months earlier, she'd told me that she and Matan were dating.

I know Sarah is thinking hard about the trip. Deliberating. She says she stopped asking but I can clearly remember her harsh statements hurled at me just a year ago when I said that, at sixteen, I left home after discovering what my father really was, and in the same breath bawled my heart out at having lost the relationship with Talya.

"You Germans," her tone had been disparaging, "do you really believe that your parents' actions will ever disappear? You fled home and said to yourself, 'OK, that's it, I've done something good and so I can be forgiven,' right? 'I'm allowed to know that Ludwig is the one who abusively toyed with Yosseleh and thousands of other Jews in Lublin,' you think to yourself, 'and just keep it to myself even though I'm simultaneously nurturing a relationship and familial closeness with Talya' who, from the day you first met her, so you yourself say, was always searching for details about the fates of her father's family members in Lublin, and particularly her cousin Yosseleh. The perfect bluff. Did you truly think that dynamite information like that would just lie dormant and never explode?"

That's what my daughter said to me. "I have not the slightest doubt that your Abba would never have let me keep those facts buried so deep," was all I could whisper back. I could hear Noah berating me through her voice. She'd bent down to hug me. On her sixteenth birthday she was once again the mother, and I was the lost girl.

No, it was time for a change. I stood, took a deep breath, and phoned Rona. I told her about the invitation, and asked her to talk to Sarah, knowing that Rona's rational mode of expression might encourage Saraleh to take a more positive view, and lead her to deciding she'd join me on this trip. Deep down I also knew that without Saraleh at my side, I'd never be able to face going to Poland.

EDWARD PERKINS-KARLINSKI
Warsaw, April 1990

Talya wrote to Christina, telling her we'd be coming to Poland and including an invitation to my lecture at Catholic University, Lublin. Christina suggested we meet with her son David in Warsaw, and together make our way to Lublin because he was also scheduled to attend the conference.

"David's a cardiologist," Talya informed me.

"And also connected to Yosseleh?" I chuckled.

Her eyes opened wide. "Yes, of course!"

She put her lemon tea down on the end of the massive desk she'd bought me as a gift after we returned to Israel. Her explanation for the purchase? "I'm enticing you with a good reason to want to work at home too, and not just in the university office," she'd grinned.

Much of the lecture I'd prepared for Lublin I actually did write at home. I described the brain of a regular guy who turns into a raving murderer, while the spirit of Yosseleh sat next to me in his torn sweater, gazing at me through his black eyes rimmed in thick lashes. Sometimes he'd be watching my face, sometimes my hand holding the silver pen, sometimes the printed pages. Sometimes I wanted to ask him to please leave, sometimes I was a little startled because he would leave and then my hand would stop writing, freezing in its place until his lovely face would spirit itself back.

But he didn't disappear. He seemed to be within me.

"I'm going with Yishai to wander around Warsaw's Old Town and Jewish Quarter," Talya says as she puts a crimson lipstick on.

"Wine red?" I wonder aloud.

"Uh-hmm, in honor of the capital city," she answers. "Sophie and Saraleh are landing in an hour. We've arranged to meet for dinner at the hotel."

"Well, I'll remind you to use that lipstick in their honor too!" I squeeze her. She gazes up at me.

"You and your silly stuff," she pretend-punches me.

"I'm meeting David at the café near Park Chopin," I let them know my plans too.

"Sounds great," Yishai says. "Maybe we'll join you later!"

Talya gives me a quick hug. "C'mon Yishai, let's go find bargains. Chopin sheet music for you and a string of amber beads for me."

I know how excited and nervous she is before this reunion with Sophie and Saraleh. I head in the direction I need to go. From the distance I see David standing at the café's entrance: a tall handsome man with gold-blond hair, dapper in a pin-striped, gray suit. As I come closer I notice the pin on his lapel: a chess knight looking for all the world like it's just taken a momentary break from a game. He really looks like a model who's stepped out of a fashion magazine.

He holds his hand out to shake mine. Talya would instantly have said his fingers are beautifully sculpted, a pianist's fingers. And his sapphire blue eyes narrow as he smiles warmly.

"I recognized you from the photo of you and Talya that my mother showed me," he says in too-perfect English with a heavy Polish accent. "I'm so pleased to meet you. I do hope you enjoy the location I picked out for you."

He leads me to a table. "To accompany our coffees, may I take the liberty of ordering a selection of the most wonderful cakes that this café is known for: napoleonskis, ponczes, and eclairs?"

"Of course! Sounds great to me!" I say, charmed by this perfect act of gentility. "I understand you're a cardiologist."

"I'm a doctor. Heart disease, not heart disease… there are so many illnesses. But it's better not to fall into the hands of doctors," he grins. "At least, that's what my teacher, Dr. Marek Idelman, the man from whom I learned everything about medicine, would always say." That angelic smile again.

"And what led you to studying under Dr. Idelman?" There it is: the question that's been rolling around my thoughts ever since the day that Christina shared certain details about David and his sphere of specialization with Talya in a letter. 'Healing hearts' is exactly how Christina worded it, Talya told me and giggled.

"My mother," he answered briefly. I noticed a film of moisture come to his eyes.

A moment of almost awkward silence ensued but right away he went back to being the perfect host. "Ah! Here's our coffee and cakes. You will never forget how they taste!" Using small tongs he placed two donut-shaped cakes and a napoleon on my plate. "These are the best to start with," he nodded knowingly.

"I wouldn't be surprised if I'd need to become one of your patients after this decadence!" I laughed.

"Oh, this once at least I permit you to be a little unserious, Dr. Perkins."

That smile again. His easygoing manner and honesty make me feel as if I've known him all my life. A long-lost brother.

"You'll be a doctor. That's what my mother always told me," he continued. "She was quite insistent about me studying with the Jewish surgeon she'd read about who operates in the Lodz Hospital on people's hearts. In our first class at Lodz University, after that statement about familiarizing with death, which of course was there for every moment of his life in the Warsaw Ghetto, Dr. Idelman explained the diagnostic method he believes in. I quote: 'A good doctor is one who, looking at a person, is reminded of something. It's not a magical or wondrous talent. You just need to know how to observe the patient and how to connect the dots.' And so, every time an intern joins my department in Lublin, that's the first thing I tell them. I stole it unapologetically from Marek."

He must certainly be an excellent teacher, I thought. And as if in answer, David continues.

"Dr. Idelman developed an original method for teaching medical students. When the patient enters the room we should make an initial diagnosis. Plunge right in and draw an instinctive diagnosis despite fears of making mistakes. That initial diagnosis would then become fertile ground for extensive discussions later. I adopted the method when I became a mentor."

I studied him: his lovely face, his smile, his fingers. When he spoke, there was no intonation of someone wanting to make an impression. He spoke calmly and articulately. Taking a bite of his éclair, he encouraged me to do the same.

"Heaven!" we both said at the same time, and laughed. Once again I had that feeling that I'm extremely familiar with David.

"Me with matters of the brain and you with matters of the heart. Well, we certainly complement each other!" I said.

David nodded, sipping from his coffee.

"My mother said that you no doubt like lemon tea, because she remembered how, in the Zilberman-Karlinski family, they always drank it in cups of the most delicate glass. So don't worry. When we get to Lublin, my mother will be thrilled to pamper you."

Then his face turned a little serious. "I haven't stopped talking. It's very impolite of me."

He looked like a little boy knowing he'll be rebuked later for misbehavior by his mother. He smiled in a bashful way. My heart skipped a beat, even though we were of similar ages, but somehow I felt he just needed a fatherly hug. Then I immediately chided myself for my patronizing attitude.

"Don't worry about it. I really enjoy listening to you," I reassured him. "I'm enjoying your openness and this feeling of being family."

His eyes opened wide. "On my third birthday, my mother whispered a secret in my ear that I never understood. 'We have good friends in Israel. They're part of our family.' I remember Stefania, my grandmother, telling her, 'Stop!' and my father, Igor, would also look annoyed. Ever since then and on every birthday, she'd whisper this secret about family in Israel. When I grew older she'd say that the day would come when they'd come here. She'd also been writing to Herman, Talya's father."

"From the first day I ever met Talya, she spoke about her cousin, Yosseleh, and also spoke about Yosseleh's best friend Christina, so it was clear that you're our Lublin connection," I said. "But tell me more about Idelman."

David took another sip before continuing. "In December 1968, a patient came to the Lodz Hospital department where Dr. Idelman worked. His heart was ruined. The only chance of saving him involved a transplant. That was just one year after Dr. Christian Barnard's successful transplant operation. As a student specializing in cardiology, I was fascinated when I watched the operations by Professor Moll and Dr. Idelman. No words could describe the excitement that gripped us all. We were part of history in the making. It was Poland's first heart transplant, and the second in the world."

"We took up observer positions behind the glass of the operating theater's door, which opens like a window especially for events such as teaching or, as became the case later on, larger scale assistance teams. Additional cardiologists stood next to us. Hematologists, immunologists, biochemists. Surgery lasted an hour. The heart pumped for an hour longer. It was stunning, extraordinary. But then problems began in the right chamber. The pressure in the blood vessels in the patient's lungs rose so high that the heart couldn't cope and burst."

"There was a heavy silence. The Professor distanced from the operating table. When I met with Dr. Idelman in his rooms after the surgery, he told me and two other interns the statements that are etched in my memory to this day and which, Eddie, I'll give you, too, as a gift. 'In medicine,' he said, 'in addition to skill you need courage. Without the transplant, it was clear that the patient would die. He did die, but we just experienced our first transplant.' And then he said, 'When you are closely familiar with death, you feel more responsible towards life. Every chance is a chance worth taking. Even the faintest chance possible is important and worthwhile.'"

David's eyes shone. Taking a tissue from his pocket, he gave his nose a very slight dab.

"I remember Viki, a friend from my summer holidays in Sydney. To this day we're friends. Every year we'd travel to visit my grandparents in Sydney. Her parents came from Poland. When I was about five, her grandfather came from Poland to visit and told us tales about Poland: the forests and rivers, and the beauty of the small Polish villages.

"But mostly he spoke about a large, important city with a port, much like that of Sydney. He called it Gdansk, an odd name to an Ozzie kid's ear. Much later I realized that it was the city where the protest against Communism began by the Solidarity Movement. I've a hunch Dr. Idelman was one of the movement's activists."

"My mother said Dr. Idelman was a Warsaw Ghetto fighter, a cardiologist, and an activist fearlessly protesting to oust the oppressive communist regime in Poland. Quite the resume," David laughed.

"As time passed, Dr. Idelman became my mother's very close friend. He knew about how she'd almost managed to save Yosseleh from the Nazis. Every time Marek was in Lublin, he'd come to visit us. She'd always ask him the same thing. 'Marek, tell us how you fought in the ghetto.' And he would describe how he would fearlessly walk right between two SS soldiers with a pistol in each hand, completely scornful towards death. He strode so boldly that the Gestapo soldiers would move away without ever realizing that the group he was leading actually had no weapons at all."

That made me think of how Viki's grandfather would chuckle. "You Ozzies," he'd say to my Dad, "haven't a clue about real life." I never understood it back then.

David suddenly stood. Turning to look in the direction of his gaze, I see Talya and Yishai entering. His smiling is guiding them to our table.

"Ah, my dears, come. Let's see the chess players near Chopin's statue in the park."

Talya gives him a warm hug. "My whole life," she says, "I've missed you."

SOPHIE MENDELSOHN:
April 1990

Right away Yishai asked Saraleh which piano piece she liked the most. "Moonlight Sonata" was her answer.

"So come with me," he said.

"We always dreamt they'd be like siblings," Talya noted. I hugged her and we stood there, in that hug, until we could feel the sounds enveloping us.

"I think there's still a chance they could be brother and sister," I said, tugging Talya towards the lobby where Yishai was playing on the grand piano.

We crept forward on tiptoe, not wanting to disturb him. Sarah, who stood next to the piano, turned her head towards us, smiled and placed a finger on her lips. The universal sign of hush.

For seventeen years we hadn't seen each other. Seventeen years in which not a day went by that Talya wasn't in my thoughts. We didn't talk about the past, or about the conversation in that Australian café. The past can be restored when the present is rebuilt and flowing smoothly. I'm sure that at some point, we will dive into the depths of our private past.

There in the hotel in Warsaw, several days before we delve back into that distant past and the darkness and difficulty of our families in Lublin, I knew we could go back to being family. I'm doing all I can to help those who suffered at the hands of my ancestors' nation, but now I know who I am:

Sophie Mendelsohn,

IDF war widow,

Mother of Sarah.

"Let's stroll arm in arm like we did in Ein Yam and leave the kids to their own devices," she invites, laughing that special laugh of hers and linking her arm with mine. "Eddie will be down from our room soon and we'll all go to eat. Christina's son David's also joining us. Remember I wrote to you about him?"

"Of course I remember. I remember everything. But will you come up with me to my room first? I've got something for you."

Opening my suitcase I pull out the box I found in the Schmidt basement, with its cache of letters from the Lublin Ghetto, the photos, the folded whip. I give everything to Talya.

"When I last visited Heidelberg after Ludwig died, my mother gave me this package, said that she's sure I'll study history, and that these documents from Germany's darkest period should be in my possession. But you're the one who researches that period and location. These documents are now yours."

Talya hugs me tight. "Thank you, my sister," she whispers.

An unfamiliar but deep tranquility wraps itself around me, a feeling of joy at the most unexpected time and place in my life.

TALYA KARLINSKY:
April 1990

The lecture over, David invited us back to his mother's house. Christina opened the heavy wooden door and greeted us.

Her beauty made my head spin. White hair down to her waist, pulled back with two large, brown clips. Eyes like massive sapphires. A wide, bright smile with perfect teeth. Poets were born to write of such beauty. If I'd have been an artist, I'd have depicted her as some kind of dreamy Venus robed in white. Two creases at the corners of her mouth, and the wrinkles on her brow, were not able to flaw her beauty.

At close to seventy, she stood straight-backed as she spoke to us. "Come, come in, my family. My beloved family. I've waited so many years for this moment."

Her eyes shone with tears. She was like a fashion mannequin but rather than wearing makeup she wore, like a Madonna, tiny teardrops.

Eddie was half comforting me and half holding me up. He could feel my whole body shaking. I could see the tears welled in the corners of Christina-Madonna's eyes, waiting for the moment of release to freely stream down her face, and our faces and those of Yishai and Sarah and Sophie who came with us to Poland to hear Eddie's lecture on "Syndrome E: The driving force behind human evil," and attend the granting of an Honoree Doctor by the Lublin University to Professor Edward Perkins-Karlinski. And of course to meet Christina and her son David.

We sipped lemon tea in the most delicate glass cups, just the way Abba would serve it. We ate apple charlotte cake with whipped cream. Heavenly! Christina spoke in measured quiet tones. Yishai and Sarah pulled their chairs closer to her.

"Ludwig went back to Heidelberg for Easter. I came on Monday, as I did every Monday, to the fortress where Yossi was imprisoned after the ghetto was eradicated."

Hearing her father's name, Sophie audibly gasped. Sarah quickly brought her water. She sipped, then clasped Sarah's hand.

In her quiet manner, Christina continued. "I was using a special permit from the municipal sanitation department, which gave me entry. I went into the main courtyard and had to go through the checkpoint. The guards weren't in their usual places. I stood behind the brown fence clutching a basket of food that I'd brought for Yosseleh. I noticed the guards and several other people watching the 'show.' My gut felt as though it would spill out through my skin and slither on the earth like great snakes. When I opened my mouth, no sound came out."

"Stockmeister stood over Yosseleh, who was prone on the ground. He was kicking Yosseleh anywhere his boot could make contact. 'Do you think you came here to play chess? Did you think it would save you, filthy zhid? Where's your Herr Schmidt savior now, huh?' he screeched in a mad frenzy, waving his pistol around."

"Yosseleh was curled up in an odd way, looking like a red ball. Blood came from everywhere. I closed my eyes and prayed for him to be released from his agony. And then… three shots. To this day I have no idea where I got the strength from not to faint on the spot and instead, tell myself to get out of there as fast as I could. I started making my way down the hill. I made it to Growdska Street and the Jewish Orphanage. After all its occupants had been murdered, the building was turned into offices. I sat on a bench in the entrance. I knew Igor worked as a cleaner there."

"Igor found me, and before I fainted I managed to tell him that Yosseleh was murdered at the Fortress and that we need to get him buried in Lublin's Kalinowszczyzna Street Old Jewish Cemetery. Later he told me that for three days I was feverish, muttering, shouting, tossing and turning. When the fever eventually dropped I asked about Yosseleh. He said that he'd found him and buried him. Four days after Yosseleh was brutally murdered, the Red Army conquered Lublin."

No one in the room moved. We barely breathed. I saw tears streaming from Christina's eyes. They seemed to mingle on the floor with mine, and those of Zeideh Karlinski, and Yosseleh's mother Hava, and his uncle Herman, and his older sister Brahaleh, but also with those of Yishai and Sarah and Eddie and Sophie and Noah, forming a great blood-red salty pool that would bury us at any moment.

"Talya! Talya!" I heard Eddie's voice from within the heavy fog.

They were laying me down on the floor. Sophie brought cushions and raised my legs. Yishai brought me a glass of water. A few minutes later I could sit up again, although my face blushed furiously from the embarrassment at fainting, and the shame: how could I have been the one collapsing from shock when Christina was the true hero.

"I'm okay," I muttered in a voice barely above a whisper. "I'm really sorry," I said, turning to Christina who smiled with her perfect, patient smile. But I could see tears still welling in her sapphire eyes. "I brought the letters that you wrote to my father after the war. I only found them after he died, and every time I intended to open the brown bag and get them translated, something held me back. I was afraid."

"It's late now, and we're all tired," Christina said. "But tomorrow morning let's visit Yosseleh's grave. By some miracle, the cemetery wasn't damaged in the bombing. As he'd asked me at the time, I had his mother's family name also engraved on the headstone in honor of his beloved grandfather, Rabbi Karlinski."

Silently we walked to the apartment Christina rented for us nearby, for the duration of our Lublin stay. At night, every time I woke, almost screaming, Eddie enveloped me in his arms, caressing me gently to calm me. 'Eddie, noblest of men' was the thought that repeatedly echoed in my mind during that difficult night of sleeping and waking.

Christina prepared breakfast for us. "Eat, Talinka,"

I could hear Abba saying in my thoughts. "You always loved the sour milk I used to buy at the Polish grocery store in Tel Aviv, and the thick slices of black bread spread with butter."

"Take slow deep breaths," Eddie said. "You need to get your strength back before we go to the cemetery."

"I can feel Herman here, Eddie."

He nods.

"We're all here," Yishai says softly.

"Abba never mentioned the letters," I tell Christina. "When he'd tuck me into bed, he always told me stories about Yosseleh, his sister Hava's son, the brilliant boy who won the Polish youth chess championship. He did say that Yosseleh had a childhood friend, the daughter of his neighbors, who he played with a lot. I found the letters among his documents. Everything was under a pile of towels that always emitted a pleasant scent because he kept slivers of soap between them."

Christina smiled. "Yosseleh wanted to study medicine and specialize in human brain research," she said. "He started talking about it after his bar mitzvah. Until then everyone was certain he'd become a great Rabbi like his grandfather."

I notice Eddie's response in his smile. I know he's thinking about the dozens of times I'd said that he, in fact, is Yosseleh, the boy from Lublin. As we walked to the Lublin Jewish cemetery, we chatted. Yishai held his notebook and every so often jotted something down. Sarah walked next to him.

"I'm so glad you're writing," I say to him on the train from Warsaw to Lublin.

"I don't want to miss a thing," he says in his now fully developed bass which charms me every time he speaks.

My Yishai, who will always be the kid with the squeaky voice, is now speaking adult thoughts in a mature voice.

The headstone is simple and bears the Hebrew inscription: "Here lies our beloved Yossef (Yosseleh) Zilberman-Karlinski son of Abraham and Hava Zilberman. Born 29 Tishrei 5686 corresponding to 17 October 1925. Murdered at the Lublin Fortress on 4 Av 5704 corresponding to 20 July 1944."

"Igor and I put the headstone up five years after the war," I heard Christina speaking so softly it was almost a whisper. "Igor buried him a day after the murder and marked the site with a wooden pole. He asked the man who guarded the nearby forest to watch over the grave. When I finally recovered, I'd come here to place violets on it, and brought two fir trees which began in small pots and now stand on either side of the grave."

We stood in a circle, listening to the birds, the cars in the distance, and every so often, a sigh from one of us. No one spoke.

"Not far from here there's a small park where we can sit for a while," David suggested.

Silently we walked there. Christina took two blankets from her tote and spread them over the stone benches beneath the large ficus tree. We sat together in a comfortable hush. David shook his head slightly, his blue eyes moist.

She must be waiting for some kind of permission from me, I thought. Suddenly she looked old, broken. No sparkling smile. No perfect teeth. The joints of Sophie's fingers were blue with the effort of holding her bag. Sarah and Yishai were looking down at their feet. Standing behind the bench, Eddie firmly gripped my shoulders. I could feel blood in my mouth: I was so tense that I'd bitten my tongue. I wanted to scream it out: Tell us, tell us everything, tell us now!

"My husband Igor was Yosseleh and my childhood friend. Although he was four years older than us, he loved joining us to play our games, especially building the snowman in the yard. His mother Stefania worked as a housekeeper for the Karlinski and Zilberman families. She was there with Hava when Yosseleh was born, and saved Hava's life after a difficult birth."

Closing her eyes, Christina fell silent. Pulling a thermos flask from his bag, David poured tea for her. Slowly she sipped and drew in a deep breath.

"Ten years ago Igor's doctors found a malignant tumor in his brain. Even though David brought the top experts from Warsaw to treat him, he died six months later. But before he died, he held my hand. 'You haven't forgotten what we agreed? You'll tell him?' he whispered."

Christina spoke in a flat monotone. "Igor was a true friend. Perhaps he also liked me, even though he knew Yosseleh and I were in love from our earliest childhood. I believe he proposed marriage because, knowing I was pregnant, he wanted to save me and Yosseleh's child. Although the war was now over, anti-Semitism did not disappear. Jews who came back to their homes faced seething hatred, and in no small number of instances, were even murdered as they stood in front of what used to be their own doorways, requesting their homes back.

Igor and I decided to raise David as our own child."

Glancing at the others, I saw eyes and mouths open wide in shock. Am I the only one, I wonder, who 'knows' the truth behind this story? Am I the only one who sees both Yosseleh and my father Herman reflected in David's eyes? Christina gazed at me before continuing.

"This is the matter I wrote to your father about. He supported our idea. David's light blue-gray eyes, which he inherited from his Karlinski grandfather and me, helped a good deal. At the time, a lot of people in the neighborhood were talking, with barely restrained glee, about how good it was that the Jews with their dark eyes had all gone from the town."

I went over to David and hugged him tight. I could feel our tears mingling as they rolled down our cheeks. Sophie, Yishai and Sarah formed an embracing circle around us. Eddie poured Christina a glass of water and held her hand.

"Herman wrote that in due time, David should be told. Every cell in my body knew, all these years, that someone from the family would arrive. And here you all are," she said softly, the beautiful smile returning to her face, signaling that she'd told all she could of what I could only think of as a dark fairytale.

"I'm going back to the grave to recite Kaddish," I said, referring to the traditional Jewish mourner's prayer.

"I'll say it with you," Yishai said.

"And I'm coming too," added David.

Sophie also joined us. Slowly, aloud, word by word, we recited the Kaddish in unison.

Sophie was already closely familiar with the Jewish

custom of placing pebbles or small stones on a grave to symbolize participation in the sacred act of burial.

Collecting several, she set them gently down on the grave of Yosseleh Zilberman-Karlinski.

∽

Printed in Great Britain
by Amazon